The Other Man

The Other Man

Shashank Kela

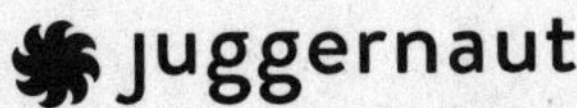

JUGGERNAUT BOOKS
KS House, 118 Shahpur Jat, New Delhi 110049, India

First published by Juggernaut Books 2017

10 9 8 7 6 5 4 3 2 1

ISBN 9789386228239

For sale in the Indian Subcontinent only

Typeset in Adobe Caslon Pro by R. Ajith Kumar, New Delhi

Printed at Manipal Technologies Ltd

For Karuna

At dawn the condemned men were let out of the guardhouse, a narrow, oblong cage in a corner of the police station. Taken into the courtyard, they stood blinking sleepily, rumpled and haggard after a cold, uncomfortable night. They had been handcuffed for the journey.

The station wagons standing in the yard were plain, without markings. One, parked against the furthest wall (which stank of piss), had mesh windows. The taller of the two prisoners flexed his shoulders and drew a deep breath, the other nodded to a man entering the gate. Policemen in plain clothes scurried in and out of the building. The light was silver, breaking into gold where the sun rose above the hills.

The unmarked vans were finally made ready. The station officer stalked into the yard, nodding curtly to one of the prisoners; the other he pretended not to see. The plain-clothes men, dark-skinned and young, huddled in small groups without speaking. A ragged boy trotted into the yard carrying a metal tray with glasses of tea. The plain-clothes men propped their guns against the wall and drank, glancing covertly at the station officer who stood to one side. The sergeant kept obsequiously at his heels. The prisoners raised their glasses awkwardly with manacled hands.

Finally, they set off.

The town dropped behind them as the convoy climbed the rolling hills. Sunlight silked the foliage; a bird signed the dipping arc of the sky. The wagon in which the prisoners sat was sandwiched between two jeeps. A policeman lit a cigarette, and the acrid smoke eddied for a moment before being sucked out of the window. One of the prisoners asked for a drag. 'Take it,' the guard said amiably.

He placed the cigarette between the prisoner's lips, where it dangled as he drew avidly upon it. After a few moments the prisoner felt dizzy and let it drop.

Some hours later, they were bumping down a dirt road enclosed by trees, thrown awkwardly against each other as the wagon jolted over the ruts. The silence became furred with tension. The policemen clutched their weapons tighter and no longer glanced at the prisoners. The road wound through the forest, skirting a village, straightening, turning again, before ending abruptly at a stream. The convoy halted and its occupants tumbled out. The station officer sent a couple of men ahead to reconnoitre – they returned with the news that the road had been swept away.

The station officer descended from his perch. The prisoners pulled themselves out of the wagon, stumbling a little. Trees towered above them, broken by sunlight.

'We'll have to walk,' the station officer said to the taller of the prisoners. His men surrounded them in a loose bunch. The party forded the stream and disappeared down the track.

Some time later there was a clatter of gunfire, audible in the village they had passed. Its inhabitants looked up nervously.

'We'll stop at Kakrana on the way back,' ordered the station officer, sweating a little but otherwise unmoved.

~

Three weeks later, on a cold winter's day in Delhi, Inspector Dayanidhi of the federal police agency entered his director's office.

'Damnable weather, isn't it?' said the director breezily. 'Sit down, have a look at this.' He pushed a file across the table.

Daya opened the file: it contained two sheets of paper. He read the signature on the first and looked up inquiringly.

'A *local* affair,' said the director, emphasizing the word 'local'. 'An encounter.'

A false one, thought Daya with habitual scepticism. 'Was it in the papers?' he asked.

'Obviously. Here in Delhi you can't shoot anyone without the press piling upon you. In the provinces they're not so cautious.'

Daya said nothing.

'A place called Kakrana,' the director went on. 'Two Maoists killed while trying to escape – at least that's the story. Unfortunately for the local police, one of them was a well-known man, an intellectual. There was a fuss, the press weighed in, and in the end the state government decided to order an inquiry. Which has been turned over to us...'

'I see,' said Daya. And already he could see truculent faces, doors slamming shut, lies building up like a wall. 'Is there any doubt that they *were* Maoists?'

'One of them was, without question. Oddly enough, it's his death that set off the furore. About the other, we don't know. That's something you'll have to find out.'

'When?'

'At once. You'll be working alone; we're short-staffed as it is.' The director looked at Daya shrewdly, drumming his fingers on the desk. 'I gather you prefer that,' he added with a hint of exasperation.

'When it's possible,' admitted Daya.

'It's possible,' echoed the director peevishly.

Daya left the office with a feeling of relief. It was his habit to gauge the amount of 'influence' that might be brought to bear upon an investigation should its direction prove unwelcome – much as an ox might gauge the weight of the load it is harnessed to pull. In this case, from the director's gnomic pronouncements, he carried away the impression that he'd been given a free hand.

Unusually for a policeman, Daya combined an acute realism about the nature of his job with an unwavering commitment to the ideal of justice. It was to pursue this ideal that he had chosen to enrol in the police rather than the administrative branch. Eight years in the job had taught him the futility of his expectations, tempered his ardour with weariness. The very qualities that made him a good detective – reticence, intelligence, a capacity for self-effacement (which prompted people to open up to him), curiosity – were all but guaranteed to make him unpopular with his colleagues. In the agency he enjoyed a reputation for intransigence in the conduct of his cases and the unambiguous clarity of his reports – a troublesome, prickly officer, but not without his uses.

Daya paused in the capital only long enough to present his credentials and obtain a copy of the case files. The officer who met him made no effort to conceal his disapproval.

'Where would we be,' he complained, 'if this happened every time the police shot someone? I don't blame you; you're only doing your job. It's the recommendation that sticks in my craw. A minor incident, two terrorists killed…a certain amount of fuss, I grant you, some bad publicity, but surely nothing to warrant a witch-hunt…'

'Those men weren't terrorists,' Daya pointed out. 'They were Maoists – there's a difference, surely.'

The officer waved the difference away. 'Terrorists, Maoists, it's all the same...I have a friend who was posted in Bastar. D'you know what it's like, driving into the jungle, not knowing when a landmine is going to blow you sky-high? They' – he jerked his thumb towards the window, from which another office block was visible – 'want us to stamp rebellion out as though it was as easy as cracking an egg...well, it can't be done, not with an inquiry ordered every time someone gets shot.'

'You think so?' Daya asked neutrally.

'I expect you'll appreciate our difficulties when you get out there and see things for yourself.'

As he had expected, the case files were thoroughly uninformative. He noted that the police party guarding the prisoners (who had been taken to Kakrana 'for purposes of further investigation') were members of a special unit, whose remit was anti-insurgency operations. Specializing, no doubt, in arm-twisting, torture, murder. All we need are paramilitaries, thought Daya with disgust. There was nothing he hated more than the conflation of the functions of policeman and executioner – embodied in 'encounter specialists' posing for photographs, smirking and cradling their pistols like babies. As for those of his colleagues (all too many) who justified these methods by citing the inadequacies of judicial procedure, he suspected them of bad faith and worse.

For what is the arbitrary power to coerce and kill but the negation of justice? Take the word '*encounter*' (a metallic taste of ashes and aloes filled his mouth) with its implication of something accidental, unplanned, contingent – in this case, a fracas in which shots are exchanged. But when accidents become routine and the results are always the same, it acquires a technical, bureaucratic connotation corresponding to its function of endowing arbitrary acts with the fig-leaf of due process. And, since even euphemism has its limits, it is at this point that it becomes hedged around with adjectives: the staged or false encounter, a theatre of death with the props carelessly arranged.

Daya tossed the file upon the table. His room smelled musty; from the window he could see a tree and a patch of sky stained with neon. In it shone a single star. The brittle roar of traffic had dwindled. He flicked off the light and stood by the window, watching the star.

~

It was still dark when he boarded the bus for Sirkhedi. The streets through which the bus nosed resembled a dreamscape, their detritus of filth and human flotsam tucked safely out of sight. Gradually the city petered out; now the lunging headlights could only pick out the grey bulk of trees, the ghostly presence of fields. The light of dawn drifted up from the ground enfolding each object like an eggshell before hardening to a dazzle. The bus kept stopping along the highway until it was full. Daya leaned back in his seat (which smelled of dust and cigarette smoke) and closed his eyes. He slept in snatches, vaguely conscious of the ruts in the road, the crush of bodies in the aisle, the raised voice of the conductor.

They stopped at a checkpoint where he got down to stretch his legs. Then for hours the bus climbed and descended a series of hills, through intervals of forest where the wind blew cold, before reaching a plateau. The landscape became wilder and more rugged. Villages emerged from the wavering line of trees and bushes, the familiar elements of houses, fences, fields arranged in strange, unfamiliar patterns. Some of the fields were slashed by enormous trenches with bones of rock jutting through. Mining pits, said the man next to him, sizing the stranger up. Dump trucks passed the bus at intervals.

Looking out of the window, Daya was transported back to the landscape of his childhood. For many years they had lived in a small town in the Deccan, where a line of hills was visible on the horizon. The front garden had a border of rosebushes. At dusk the roses would gather up the light as the statuary of trees dissolved around them. And when the roses were finally quenched, the bland moon would shed its indifference and begin to glow.

They reached Sirkhedi at midday. Daya groggily picked his way through the rubbish in the square where the bus disgorged its passengers. The thread-like lanes leading from it were crammed with shops and kiosks. At the blind end, above a retaining wall, rose the crumbling facade of an old fort. Crossing the square, Daya entered the first lodging house that he saw. He wrote his name in the register, putting 'Delhi' in the column marked 'Coming From'. After the completion of these indispensable formalities he was shown into a tiny cubicle. He washed his face, changed his shirt and came down again. The receptionist directed him to a restaurant nearby.

After eating, he wandered aimlessly up a street lined with rickety buildings set flush against each other, without a chink of light in between. Gradually the shops thinned out, a small temple appeared, then workshops, offices, the wall of a school, a junction. Daya turned right. After a while the road divided again – the branch road had an arch at its mouth to underscore its significance. A sign announced the way to the pilgrim shrine which was Sirkhedi's chief claim to fame. Obediently, Daya followed the sign. The town seemed to peter out into patches of wasteland and fields, only to reappear abruptly – houses and shops, empty lots, a yard packed with dump trucks. Next to it loomed the wall of the shrine, spires visible above it. The entrance was a narrow gateway opening into a large flagstone courtyard.

It took Daya a little while to realize that the original temple had been relegated to a corner, usurped by an unfinished concrete building with giant plaster idols flanking the doorway. For all our boasts of antiquity, he thought, we don't like its remains: stone is quickly painted over, frescoes whitewashed, new shrines built to replace the old. To the superfluity of ancient temples, promptly abandoned when those who commissioned them are dead, we add new ones, ugly where their predecessors had at least been beautiful. As was this temple, despite the fact that its stone was pitted and eroded, the carvings worn away.

He peered over the rear wall, standing on tiptoe. It abutted a river whose dimpled surface was covered with rotting flowers, incense sticks, all the usual paraphernalia of worship. An expanse of scrub scored by narrow paths separated it from higher ground. A door in the wall opened to a small bridge; on the other side rose a huddle of buildings stacked tightly against each other. A rich endowment, he thought idly, to have a bridge built especially for it.

Daya crossed the courtyard and walked back to the hotel. Ten minutes later there was a peremptory knocking on the door of his room. He opened it to find two policemen standing outside. Roughly, they demanded to see his identification.

~

The station officer sat behind his desk, hands folded over the shelf of his belly. The windows of his room opened into the courtyard; a curtained doorway led to the outer office where the constables sat. One was standing by the door, watching them with the strained attentiveness of a hunting dog. When Daya lit a cigarette, he hurried over to place an ashtray on the desk. Daya thanked him courteously.

'You have an efficient system of informers,' Daya remarked.

'This is a disturbed area…we like to keep an eye upon strangers.'

'It must be difficult to sort out the suspicious characters from pilgrims.'

The station officer steepled his fingers judiciously. 'I wouldn't say that. The pilgrims don't come from too far afield…it's the look that counts if you take my meaning. The hotel owners have instructions to report anyone who looks suspicious to us – people with city clothes, strange accents…'

'Do you see many of them here?'

'Not more than usual, no,' said the station officer. Something about Daya's unruffled demeanour was making him uneasy. Mentally he cursed his luck.

'What do people hereabouts think of the Maoists?' asked Daya.

The station officer emerged from his gloomy reflections. 'This is a small town. The mining company. The temple. Shops, traders, farmers… the temple's head priest is a good man, a power in these parts. Naturally he hates the Maoists' guts. The respectable element is terrified of them and more than happy to cooperate…'

'How long have you been working here?'

'Twelve years.'

'That's a long time. Obviously your superiors think highly of you.'

'The job is nothing but trouble,' the station officer said vindictively. 'Your inquiry for instance... Well, I do the best I can – which is not to say I don't wish they'd find someone else to do it...'

'Then you've nothing to worry about,' Daya remarked.

'Eh? I'm just letting off steam. If you were in my place, you'd do the same I expect...no offence meant.'

'Right,' said Daya amiably. 'I'll have to question you formally, but not now, later. Right now, I need a place to stay. Where is the circuit house?'

'I'll ring them up,' the station officer offered. Without waiting for a reply, he picked up the phone. After a brief conversation, he hung up beaming. 'There you are, it's all arranged...a nice place, near the river. I'll have you dropped there... no, not at all, it's my pleasure.'

~

The circuit house was shabby and dilapidated, with an overgrown garden sloping down to the river. The caretaker's family lived in a corner of the yard. After unpacking, Daya went for a walk. A man was wading across the river – apart from his silhouette the landscape seemed deserted. The sun had set, the light was fading. What remained of the day was enfolded by the water, which held up the light in sheets of silver before letting it sink. When the last glow had faded from its surface, Daya turned back to where the pitched roof of the circuit house loomed like a tent above the garden.

He ate dinner in a bare room illuminated by two unshaded light-bulbs. It was served by the caretaker, a scrawny, middle-aged man. His son went to school and his oldest daughter had just got married. He complained about his pay, which was low because he hadn't yet been 'made permanent'. Someone in the district commissioner's office had promised to get this done; when Daya inquired how much the favour would cost, he looked embarrassed and remained mute. His wife was on the payroll too, though, like him, on contract. As for the town, it still did some trade thanks to pilgrims visiting the temple, but, for the rest, things were going downhill. No one ventured into the countryside after dark, that was when all the buses stopped. A few months ago, the Maoists had blown up one of the mining company's depots. In the jungle they did what they pleased, for the forest guards had stopped their customary patrols. If they ventured out it was only during the day, and who could blame them? As for the local people, it was difficult to make out what they thought; whether they were afraid of the Maoists or hand in glove with them – a bit of both probably. A few had become civilized, but as for the rest – well, the inspector would see for himself. Most of them wore clothes now, some had become Christians, but still... The caretaker shook his head. It takes more than one bath to wipe off the stink of generations of barbarism. They still carry bows and arrows and their women copulate with any man who takes their fancy, like bitches in heat...

'I bet plenty of people cut deals with the Maoists,' Daya interrupted. 'Contractors and bus owners, the mining company...'

The caretaker looked away. 'What can a poor man say?' he said finally. 'These are matters for... others.' Using a word that signified both *'higher-up'* and *'socially superior'*. 'Sometimes one has to be...flexible.'

~

The station officer was truculent and nervous. The door to the outer room had been closed. A procession of constables knocked, entered, saluted. He signed papers and barked instructions, seemingly oblivious of Daya's presence. When the last man had left, he turned to him, laying his hands on the table as if to say: Now what can I do for *you*?

Daya stubbed his cigarette out. 'Do you know,' he began conversationally, 'that there's a proposal to outlaw smoking in public places? Other countries have laws like that apparently… When I think about it, I'm torn between my approval on principle and my predicament as a smoker. Not to mention my sovereign right to poison myself if I feel like it. They say one should give it up and they're right – cancer is no joke – but personally I've never felt any inclination to try.'

The station officer blinked.

'When did you arrest them?' Daya went on amiably.

'Who?' the station officer asked, confused by the sudden change of subject.

'These two.' Daya tapped the file in front of him.

'I arrested only one of them.'

Daya consulted his notes. 'You mean Stephen Murmu?'

'That's right.'

'Murmu was picked up first, Shanker later… Tell me about them.'

'Well, Shanker's arrest – that's not his real name, by the way – was something of a coup. He was the highest-ranked Maoist we've captured in these parts. The other man was a born troublemaker–'

'What were they charged with?'

'Hold-ups, extortion, murder. There was an ambush in which a policeman was killed some years ago – it happened in Kakrana... With Shanker we didn't need much evidence: his position spoke for itself. As for the other man, I had an informer's report tying him to the ambush. Obviously we never got to the stage of filing a charge sheet in court...'

'You keep saying "the other man". But he has a name.'

'Sure,' said the station officer indifferently. 'What difference does that make? He was a Maoist.'

'Shanker was a Maoist too.'

'That's different...he wasn't a savage, he was educated.'

'Like you and me?'

'You perhaps,' the station officer said maliciously. 'But not me...not everyone is lucky enough to go to university.'

'You think so? It seems to me that almost everyone in India goes to university – even waiters and taxi drivers – but to very little effect. What about Stephen Murmu? Was he educated?'

'He was a lawyer.'

'So he was educated. What made you suspicious of him?'

'He would appear in court for Maoists we picked up. Sometimes a lawyer came down from the capital, but Murmu did all the actual work.'

'That was his job surely.'

'To defend Maoists? I don't think so. We have lawyers more patriotic than that. They wouldn't touch those cases…'

'Maybe that's why Murmu took them. What else?'

'He was involved with an outfit that went around stirring people up against mining…it claims to be peaceful but everyone knows it's a front for the Maoists. He'd go during the day to make speeches in villages where they'd come at night…a dangerous man, a born troublemaker.'

'I'm talking about evidence.'

'From what Murmu let slip we established that he'd been in touch with Shanker.'

'Is there a record of the interrogation?'

'Not of that kind of interrogation, no. But Murmu confessed that he'd visited Kakrana in order to reconnoitre the ground for the ambush. Not just a verbal confession, mind you – he signed it.'

'How was Shanker arrested?'

'We nabbed him through an informer's tip-off. Useful men, informers…he got wind of a meeting, an important one. We laid a trap. There was shooting. Unfortunately most of them got away. But not Shanker.'

'Were they remanded to judicial custody?'

You know the answer as well as I do, thought the station officer. In the confused jumble of his thoughts, rage – and alarm – rose steadily, like mercury in a thermometer. Aloud, he said: 'Only Murmu; Shanker was killed before we could produce him in court.'

Daya consulted his notes again. 'Shanker's real name was Roshan Ghandy, is that right?'

'Yes.'

'An interesting coincidence,' Daya remarked. 'I suppose he didn't want to spell it the same way.'

'What way?'

'Gandhi, Mahatma Gandhi.'

'Ghandy, Gandhi... how the hell does it matter?'

'Maybe you're right. Why did you take them to Kakrana?'

'That's where the ambush occurred.'

'So?'

'I wanted to break down their denials by confronting them with the informer's evidence.'

'Denials you hadn't been able to shake until then...who interrogated them?'

'I questioned Murmu personally.'

'And Shanker?'

'He didn't come under my jurisdiction. They questioned him in Badalpur, where the superintendent sits. I attended some of the sessions.'

'How long did you keep Murmu in custody?'

'I'll have to check…about a week maybe?'

'And after that?'

'Once the preliminary hearing was over, he was shifted to the high security prison where we usually keep Maoists.'

'And all this happened before you nabbed Ghandy?'

'Yes,' the station officer said reluctantly.

'How long was he there before you took him out again for questioning?'

'I don't know – a fortnight maybe.'

'Who decided to take them to Kakrana?'

The station officer licked his lips. 'I signed the application,' he said finally. 'But it was decided in consultation with the superintendent, you understand. And others.'

'Who were the others?'

'You'll have to ask the superintendent that.'

'When were they brought here?'

'On 28 November.'

'How long did you keep them?'

'Just one night…to get an escort ready.'

'A special unit?'

'That's right.'

'What's special about it?'

'They're recruits with advanced training in automatic weapons, interrogation techniques, jungle warfare, things like that…'

'But placed under the regular chain of command?'

'Mostly...some officers have special responsibilities.'

'Like you?'

'You could say that.'

There was a pause. Daya rose to his feet and walked to the window. The station officer watched him mistrustfully, like a gambler studying a deck of cards. Daya turned around.

'All right,' he said in the same neutral, absent-minded tone. 'Tell me what happened in Kakrana.'

Here we go, thought the station officer.

'It's simple enough…we headed for the spot where the ambush had occurred. The road had been swept away during the rains. There's a vantage point – I posted a guard there and sent some men into the valley to keep watch in that direction…I waited until they reached their positions before starting down with the prisoners. There were four of us. The firing began when we reached the bottom. We dropped to the ground; it was then that Murmu and Shanker bolted–'

'Where to?'

'Towards their comrades obviously.'

'Straight into the crossfire?'

'Maybe they thought their friends could shoot straight… Anyway, we fired to stop them. Under the circumstances, it wasn't possible to aim carefully.'

'Go on.'

'My men came up soon afterwards…I thought of outflanking the motherfuckers, but it would have been too dangerous. They know the jungle like the back of their hands. Besides, there's the danger of landmines…no, I figured the best thing was to withdraw in good order.'

'How did the Maoists learn of your plans?'

The station officer shrugged. 'They have informers too...'

'What about Murmu and Ghandy? How did they know that an attempt to rescue them would be made that day?'

'Maybe they did, maybe they didn't. It wasn't hard to figure out what was happening.'

'How strong was your case – the case against them, I mean?'

'Your guess is as good as mine. In a courtroom there's no such thing as watertight evidence. You know how it goes...'

'No, I don't,' Daya said. 'I'll need the case papers,' he went on. 'Everything you've got: witness statements, confessions, police diaries. Also the name of every policeman who was there that day, along with rank and length of service. And I'd like to go to Kakrana, to see the place for myself. When can it be arranged?'

'We'll see,' the station officer said blandly. 'These things take time. Some of the documents are in Badalpur...we'll need an escort to get to Kakrana. Why don't you write out an official request?'

~

'He's just left – after interrogating me like a suspect, a common criminal. The man means trouble, nothing but trouble...I knew it the moment I clapped eyes upon him.'

'Relax,' the voice at the other end of the line said soothingly. However, it only inflamed the station officer's anger, his simmering sense of grievance.

'That's easy to say...you're not here.'

'Trouble can be managed.'

'Why couldn't you prevent him from being sent down in the first place?' the station officer demanded resentfully.

'That wasn't possible, unfortunately...'

'He's not biting, he made it quite clear, the bastard... You should have heard his tone, his questions.'

'So?'

'With a man like that, there's no knowing where we might end up.' The 'we' was the closest the station officer dared come to a threat.

'Relax,' the voice said again. 'D'you think we're sleeping on the job? Keep your end up, make sure there's nothing for him to find.'

'I'll see to it all right,' the station officer raged. 'I'll obstruct him in spades, the son of a bitch. He wants to go to Kakrana – well, he'll get there when I'm good and ready.'

'No, take him there, give him what he wants. Get him out of there as quickly as possible.'

'You don't mean that,' the station officer said, deflated.

'Just get him out of there,' the voice repeated. 'We'll take care of the rest.'

'You should've heard him, the way he spoke. It's enough to make a man's blood boil. With anyone else, I'd have answered with my fists. Or worse…'

'Forget that. Keep your mind upon the job.'

'I'll see to it,' promised the station officer.

~

Two days later Daya found himself sitting in an unmarked jeep, staring at the back of the station officer's head. The morning was cloudy and cool, the traffic sparse – trucks, a few buses and jitneys, cyclists who jinked nervously to the side of the road when they caught sight of their cavalcade. Two vans escorted them – the station officer broke his gloomy silence only to instruct the driver to hurry up whenever the leading one passed out of sight.

They paused at a turn-off to allow the trailing van to catch up. Daya got down to stretch his legs. His example was followed by the policemen in the leading van, who promptly began milling around a teashop. The station officer remained in his seat, morosely chewing a toothpick. He gave the order to start as soon as the second van appeared. The men bolted their tea and scrambled to their seats as quickly as they could.

They turned into a dirt track hemmed with trees. It skirted a stream; the foliage thinned, huts and fields appeared.

'Kakrana,' the station officer said laconically.

They had scarcely passed the huts when the track broke up. The leading van halted. The station officer squirmed impatiently as the sergeant came up to report that they could go no further.

'There's been a mistake,' he said abruptly.

'That's right,' affirmed a constable who had drifted up with the sergeant. 'We came here afterwards–'

The station officer cut him off brusquely. 'Turn around,' he ordered.

The command was relayed to the trailing van, which began to back and fill. When the convoy was finally pointing back the way it had come, Daya asked no one in particular: 'Why don't I see anyone?'

And indeed, the village seemed deserted.

'It's a busy time,' one of the policemen replied with a tentative glance at the station officer's head. 'They're probably getting the harvest in…'

They recrossed Kakrana and plunged into a maze of clearings. The leading van halted – its driver poked his head out and looked back timidly. The sergeant got out again and trotted towards them. The station officer cursed under his breath and drummed the dashboard in exasperation.

'Are we lost again?' he inquired sarcastically. The sergeant looked down unhappily. Just then a jitney chugged around the bend towards them and stopped.

'Ask him,' ordered the station officer.

The sergeant saluted and scurried off. Daya followed slowly. The driver had already taken the sergeant to one side, to show him the way. His companion, a middle-aged peasant with a furrowed face, glanced at Daya nervously.

'Do you live in Kakrana?' Daya asked.

Yes, he did. So did the driver; the truck belonged to him. They made a trip to town every week to buy merchandise. No, there wasn't any school here: the nearest one was eight kilometres away as the crow flies. Some children studied there, some boarded in Sirkhedi. The harvest was middling this year, nothing much to speak of...

The driver returned and clambered behind the wheel. 'We've got to show them the way,' he said resignedly. The sergeant beckoned urgently to Daya.

From there it was smooth sailing. The jitney guided them through an almost invisible track to yet another dirt road. Kakrana lay out of sight somewhere on the left. These are forest roads, remarked the station officer. Fallen into disrepair because of the Maoists – the forest department is too scared to rebuild them.

As though in confirmation, they juddered to a halt. The policemen disembarked and fell into a semblance of marching order. Fording the stream, they climbed a rocky incline and emerged on to the road again.

'A benighted place,' the station officer said distastefully.

'Clearly there are people who feel at home here...'

The station officer grunted. 'It gives me the creeps. If I had my way, I'd cut the jungle down. No jungle, no Maoists – it's as simple as that.'

'What do you think keeps them going?'

'Perversity,' the station officer said. 'Depravity… the most you can say about their leaders is that they're educated and actually believe their misbegotten ideas. The rest are no better than monkeys, barbarians who don't even know what civilization means. Whose fault is it if they can't get ahead – with all the handouts the state gives them?'

Daya allowed the conversation to lapse. The policemen separated into little groups, plodding slowly, glancing warily around them. To Daya, his surroundings, down to the smallest detail – wildflowers, leaf litter, the varying colour of trees, the subtle texture of bark and leaf – seemed alive and beautiful, a source of delight marred only by the sight of his companions. Their figures awakened a faint premonitory chill, like the foretaste of death.

The road ended abruptly in an escarpment

overlooking a shallow valley. Daya could see a white line of water tumbling down on the other side. This was where he had posted a guard, explained the station officer, to keep an eye on the road; another party of men had been sent down the valley to watch the approaches from that side. But the Maoists must have taken up their positions in advance. The prisoners were led down that path on the left…

'Did you have a guide?' Daya asked.

'Yes,' the station officer said automatically.

'You mean with you?'

'No, I sent him with the other men to show them the way.'

'Who was he?'

'A villager,' the station officer said dismissively. 'We'll find him for you…someone is bound to remember his face.'

A slip, Daya thought; one that can't be covered up or, like a man, erased.

'Let's go down,' he said aloud.

'Sure,' said the station officer. 'The sergeant will

take you…if you don't mind, that is,' he added as an afterthought.

The sergeant stepped forward with an air of resignation.

Daya looked at the policemen. 'How many of you were here that day?' he asked conversationally.

Slowly, reluctantly, eight men raised their hands.

'Who accompanied the prisoners?'

One man – the fresh-faced youngster who had approached their jeep in Kakrana. His name was Surab Singh M'ta.

'He had better come with us,' Daya remarked to the station officer, who nodded sullenly and added two more to the party. The sergeant led the way down the ridge. The path, clearly marked along its spine, became fainter as they descended, more encroached with vegetation. A trail branched off at one place going uphill. The sergeant, slow and leaden-footed, cursed as he negotiated the steepest bits. M'ta muttered an occasional warning under his breath where branches whipped across the path.

They paused at the bottom to catch their breath.

'Wasn't there water here?' the sergeant asked, panting.

'No,' said M'ta. 'Further ahead.'

They went on. A few minutes later, the sergeant halted, looking around uncertainly.

'This is the place,' he said.

They were standing on level ground with a thin scattering of trees. The ridge lay behind them; to the left rose a hill bathed in sunlight. In front the path wound into the forest. A stream, partly masked by bushes, flowed to one side.

'All right,' said Daya. 'Tell me how it happened.'

They'd been walking down this path, the sergeant explained. He and M'ta were leading the way, with the prisoners in the middle and the commandant bringing up the rear. Suddenly there was a burst of gunfire.

'From where?'

The direction of the hill. Naturally they dived for cover; when they looked up, the prisoners had taken to their heels.

'Where did you aim?' Daya asked M'ta, but it was the sergeant who replied: 'At the prisoners first, to stop them from getting away. Then towards that clump of trees over there, where the firing came from…'

'Did you hit them?' he asked M'ta again.

This time the reply was immediate: No, he had aimed into the trees.

'Were their hands tied?'

No, they had been untied for the descent.

'How long did the firing continue?'

'Difficult to say…' The sergeant again. 'We kept our heads down until the others arrived. Then a man crawled through the undergrowth to check if the prisoners were alive. Finally the commandant gave the order to retreat. The bodies were manhandled into cover, then up the path – the devil's own business, that…'

'Why did you stop at Kakrana on the way back?'

'We didn't,' said the sergeant.

'I thought you did,' Daya said to M'ta.

'No,' he replied lamely.

Daya walked to the grove, leaving the others behind. Unfamiliar trees rose around him. A bird called, a leaf drifted slowly to the ground. Drops of sweat trickled down his back. The hills in the distance had turned blue in the afternoon haze.

'Let's go,' he said, returning.

~

A story full of holes, reflected Daya, despite the care taken to touch it up. It seemed clear, for example, that Murmu's confession had been extracted under torture. As for 'Shanker' or Ghandy, the likelihood was that he had been marked for execution from the very beginning – presumably that was why he wasn't produced before a judge. But why kill Murmu too: that was the question. For the moment Daya was working on the assumption that Murmu was not a Maoist. Nothing that the station officer had said contradicted this assumption – therefore some other connection existed between the two men, some other reason to want them both dead.

All these inferences and questions passed rapidly through Daya's mind as he gazed out of the window – they were born of innate scepticism and a highly developed imaginative capacity, which sometimes dealt him the wrong hand. More often than not, the inspector tended to rely upon some intangible element in order to make up his mind: the station officer's face, the intonation of his voice, his behaviour towards his subordinates. ('For Rogas, having the man before him, talking to him, getting to know him, counted more than clues – more than facts, even': Leonardo Sciascia, *Equal Danger*). The next stage was to construct a plausible hypothesis and set about testing it.

The next morning Daya hired a taxi to take him back to the capital. He got off at the railway station, and after the taxi was out of sight, hailed a rickshaw to take him to an academic institution run by the Jesuits (he had taken the precaution of looking it up while in Delhi). The history of the Catholic Church in this region went back more than a century – from the very beginning the bulk of its converts had been hill people, adivasis. After booking a room in the institute's guest house, Daya headed to the library, where he immersed himself in a mass of books and pamphlets, emerging after two days with a name and a telephone number.

Ringing up the number, he asked for Sudha K. The answer was concise – she was usually in her office between ten and one; no appointment was necessary. He took a rickshaw to the address, in a rundown apartment block, its stairwell black with the accumulated grime of years. A young man with a wall eye opened the door. 'Sudha K.? Yes, she's here,' he said, and waved Daya inside without further ado.

The front room was crammed with books and papers. Posters were pasted on the walls, newspaper cuttings and pamphlets fastened to a pinboard. Through a curtained doorway he could see an inner room with mattresses stacked in a corner, and a disordered kitchen.

Sudha K. was a tall woman with a pleasant smile imbued with a tinge of irony. A look of surprise crossed her face when Daya introduced himself.

'What can I do for you?'

Daya held up a booklet he'd brought along. 'I believe you wrote this,' he said.

'I helped write it, yes,' she said. 'But I scarcely expected the police to take account of it.'

'I'm interested.'

'I see.' She looked at him searchingly. 'I knew, of course, that the case had been turned over to the agency, but frankly one doesn't expect much.'

'On the principle that birds of a feather tend to stick together?'

'That's one way of putting it.'

'I've spoken to the station officer; I found his story unconvincing. Therefore I'm looking for other sources of information – including your organization's report on the encounter.'

'There isn't much to add to it. No Maoists came to Kakrana that day. The villagers deny it – off the record, of course – and so does the party. We spoke to people who were there at the time. We didn't print their names and I doubt if they'd be willing to testify, but there it is.'

'What was the motive?'

'To display the bodies as a token of success. To prove that anti-insurgency operations, conducted at great expense, with great brutality and inefficiency, have tangible results. Perhaps you should take a close look at the station officer's record. He's said to be in the pocket of the mining company; he's very friendly with the head priest of the temple, who's implicated in all kinds of shady dealings. He's been in Sirkhedi forever, pulled strings to avoid being transferred out. His political connections are excellent.'

'I was going to ask you about the company. Its operations seem…disruptive.'

'It's open-cast mining. They rip off the soil, down to a certain depth, and sift it for ore. Naturally the damage is considerable. It's a profitable business, new concessions have been granted.'

'So the company isn't popular?'

'Far from it…but it's a power in those parts.

Officials do what it says: it has a clandestine payroll to make sure of that.'

'What about the Maoists? Don't they have any objections?'

'As to that, your guess is as good as mine.'

'They seem to have routed the forest department,' Daya pointed out.

'Perhaps there are other considerations.'

'Let me guess…the company pays protection money.'

'Something like that. It would find it difficult to operate otherwise. Its machinery can be blown up, its workers attacked – these things happen.'

'So everyone is happy,' said Daya thoughtfully. 'How do the Maoists explain themselves?'

'They don't. The explanations, such as they are, are informal: the party needs funds to operate, build up its organization.'

'I see,' Daya said. 'What do you think of the Maoists?'

'That's not important.'

'Forgive me if it sounds impertinent, but I'd like to know – out of curiosity, pure and simple.'

'Curiosity? In my experience, it's hardly ever disinterested or simple, not in this country at any rate. But I'll tell you. Let us say that I disagree with them on pragmatic grounds because I think they're fighting a war that can't be won. And, personally speaking, because I dislike violence – as a woman, I'd say, because women know more about it than men, only there are plenty of women fighting on their side.'

'Thank you,' Daya said sincerely. 'Could you tell me a bit more about Ghandy?'

'He graduated from a well-known university, one that still counts for something. He was a scholar. It turned out that he'd written, under his nom de guerre, a book of history that was well received. A young man with brilliant prospects who threw them up to become a revolutionary. A lot of people who don't agree with the Maoists were horrified at the way he was killed – like cutting an animal's throat.'

'And the other man, Stephen Murmu – he attracted no attention?'

'Not really.'

'What's happening in Sirkhedi?'

'There are rumours of murky deals, internecine fighting. Some villagers are organizing against mining, if only in a small way. Murmu was involved in that.'

'Do you believe he had any connection with the party?'

'I don't think so. As a lawyer, he'd defend men accused of being Maoists from time to time. But I've heard that he could be critical of the party in private.'

'You've been very helpful. Is there anyone who might know more?'

'They're unlikely to want to talk.'

'Still.'

'I can put you in touch with someone,' Sudha K. said finally. 'He's the editor of a literary magazine, a

Marxist, a theoretician. I can ring him up, reassure him you're not a spy. The rest is up to you.'

~

The day was beginning in a haze of dust. Far beyond the perimeter of the garden, clouds of dust hung in the air, rising from gashed hillsides, levelled ridges, vast pits. Excavators paused for a moment to rest, metal insects in a Martian landscape, before their treads began churning again. In the mansion a man emerged from a bedroom, straightening his tie.

'Who is it?'

'B.S.K.'

'Give it to me,' and he took the phone with a contemptuous glance at the man scurrying beside him.

'It's me…how are things? … Bad, bad – well, they could be better. Yes, I know, the lawyers told me. But don't worry, it's only – what d'you call it – a temporary setback. I'm working on it – all we need is the right kind of judge. I'll call you if I need the old man's help… Meanwhile, this business becomes less profitable by the day – well, only a bit, but the problems… Whereas with that new lease…it needs investment, but you and I, we can take care of that, and the returns, long term I mean, well, there's no comparison. Besides, we need to diversify, we really do…that's why I'm counting on you. Only yesterday, I said to Arun… Arun? He's all right; he's busy with the lawyers, Sridhar's bail hearing comes up tomorrow… Things have come to a pretty pass when a member of parliament can be arrested like that, but I'll nail the chief minister, that son of a bitch, if it's the last thing I do… Yes, we made him, the bastard, and now he's trying to kick away the ladder he climbed up on…some people have no morality, no sense of gratitude. Not like your father and I, you know how far back we go, I'll remember him until my dying day… Now, listen, about this affair…yes, I know, but this inspector, the agency, I don't like it… The company's been set up, the shares transferred. That's the other thing: I need help, things aren't rosy here, I've had to make a lot of outlays… The problem is publicity, that's why I'm warning you; look at Sridhar. Anyway, I've learned my lesson. Fortunately Sridhar is as tough as they come: he even shrugs off a stint in prison – that's friendship for you, that's loyalty… Be careful, that's all I wanted to say…I know, I know…I'll see you in a few days.'

He put the phone in his pocket. 'That's it,' he said, half to himself, then more briskly: 'Where's the chopper? Have you told them to get it ready?'

'It's ready.'

'Breakfast then and we leave. Is there anything else?'

'There was a phone call for you…a woman called Jaya.'

'How did she get my number? I remember now, I gave it to her at that party in Goa. Have you heard of her? No? A model apparently, small-time but pretty…'

~

Roshan Ghandy's parents lived in a middle-class suburb, in an unostentatious house with a small garden. The door was opened by an old man who shook hands with strained courtesy and an expression of mingled vexation and hope. In the interval between greeting them and sitting down, Daya became conscious of the atmosphere of waiting, of baffled incomprehension, that seemed to permeate the house.

Roshan had been the younger child; the other, a daughter, lived in America and was 'doing well'. The children had been no trouble when young, none at all. The father was a civil servant; the mother worked as a schoolteacher. Roshan graduated from college with a degree in history. His father urged him to register for a PhD, and for that he chose to go to Delhi. Meanwhile his sister had married a doctor living in the US whose parents made no difficulties about the dowry.

Roshan enrolled for his doctoral degree. Won a scholarship. They gathered that he dabbled in politics and was well liked. They saw him during the holidays. Once, he stayed for several months in order to finish his thesis. He rarely asked for money. His parents fretted about his refusal to find a job, get married. His father retired. Then, five years ago, they received a letter – in it Roshan announced that he had joined the party and was going underground. He might not be able to meet them again; he sent his love to his sister and her family.

The letter was a short one. It left his parents bewildered and frightened – frightened for him and bitterly ashamed. Naturally they hid the truth – not just for his safety, but also to cover up their shame. When their daughter visited, the subject was never brought up. Her husband, a professional man and a naturalized American (thus doubly horrified at the idea of his brother-in-law being a communist, a revolutionary), pretended that he didn't exist.

Then, a little more than a month ago, the phone rang and a voice from out of their nightmares announced that Roshan had been arrested. The old man went through the whole gamut of his connections – retired officials, judges, friends of friends – trying to obtain permission to meet him. But no record of the arrest existed. They met a lawyer: it was not his fee that deterred them but the way he spoke, his chilly indifference. Clearly the normal rules – or what passed for normal – no longer applied. They went to another lawyer (the voice on the phone had alluded to dire possibilities): a young man with experience in fighting cases of this kind. He agreed to leave for Badalpur as soon as possible.

On Sunday the phone rang – the same voice, or perhaps a different one, told them that Roshan had been killed. Dumbly they switched on the television set and there it was, in the news.

What about the funeral? That was the first question – the old man in particular could scarcely think beyond it. The lawyer left for Sirkhedi; meanwhile they attended a demonstration in the city, listening to the speeches with bowed heads. Journalists and TV cameras arrived; they were asked to address the gathering. Finally, the mother rose to speak disjointedly, less about the son she remembered than the symbol he had been reduced to.

The lawyer rang up; the police were refusing to let him see the body. In the evening a delegation met the chief minister, who assured them in a nasal, bad-tempered monotone that he would 'ascertain the facts'. The parents went home to wait. The next day they were summoned to police headquarters and told that Roshan's corpse had been cremated secretly 'to avoid public disorder'. The remains were handed to them in a sack. They carried it home, tormented by the suspicion that the ashes might not be his after all. After a few weeks, it was announced that an official inquiry would be conducted into the circumstances of the 'encounter'. Now all their hopes, said the mother tremulously, were invested in him.

Daya listened in silence. When they had finished, he thanked them politely and said that he would keep them informed of the progress of his investigation.

'Do you–' Mr Ghandy began anxiously and broke off.

'They killed him in cold blood,' the mother put in quickly, nervously. 'Don't you agree?'

'It's a real possibility, yes.'

Find out who killed our son – if they did not say it, their silence said it for them. But truth and justice are two different things. The truth, thought Daya, should not be too difficult to uncover. He had a deep-rooted conviction in the incompetence of the police, an incompetence stemming from the belief (infallibly absorbed by each recruit and officer) that they were entitled to ride roughshod over anyone without money or connections. This belief made them careless, and it was this carelessness that Daya trusted to lead him to the truth. But justice is a different matter altogether.

Daya spent the rest of the day rereading *The Charterhouse of Parma* and pursuing the chain of associations it evoked. Stendhal's mordant portrait of the duke – consumed with terror, peering under his bed every night in fear of assassins. Montaigne's dictum that cruelty derives from fear, that too much zeal for revenge denotes cowardice, that torture, always and everywhere, is immoral. On anger:

'There is no passion that so shakes the clarity of our judgment as anger. No one would hesitate to punish with death a judge who had condemned his criminal through anger. Why is it any more permissible for fathers and schoolmasters to whip and chastise children when they are in anger? It is no longer correction, it is vengeance. Chastisement takes the place of a medicine for children, and would we tolerate a doctor who was incensed and angry with his patient?'

Thus joining small things to great and showing their importance.

He remembered his schooldays when everything had been done by rote, habit, reflex, in an atmosphere of indifference and apathy.

Ineffectively – since most children did not learn, or learned, above all, to conform. Montaigne's sceptical humanism, Stendhal's laser-beam sense of the mutability of human behaviour...his thoughts were interrupted by a telephone call. His appointment with Sudhir Pathak had been fixed for the next day.

~

Daya woke in the morning feeling feverish and unwell. He forced himself to drink a cup of coffee and eat an omelette before hailing a taxi. The address was a suburb in the outskirts of the city, where the taxi promptly plunged into a maze of identikit houses and streets resembling each other, as though sandwiched between a pair of folding mirrors endlessly repeating their reflections. In the end they had to flag a scooter down: its rider obligingly explained how to get to their destination. Daya asked the driver to wait, he'd be back in an hour.

A servant opened the door and ushered him into a room furnished with cane chairs, a table and a glass-fronted cupboard in which some journals were arranged. Daya was examining them when a man entered the room. Though neither especially tall nor stout, he conveyed an impression of size and solidity, a frigid, austere calm. Daya introduced himself and lapsed almost unconsciously into silence – the fever was spreading like a dark tide through his body.

Sudhir Pathak asked the servant to get some tea. 'There's no milk, I'm afraid,' he said in an aside to Daya. Then: 'Sudha told me about you.'

'I went to her in search of information.'

'And did you obtain it?'

'Partly, yes…she thought you might be able to help.'

'How?'

'I want to know a bit more about the Maoists.'

Sudhir Pathak looked amused. 'I'm the editor of a literary journal.'

'But you're also what used to be called a man

of the left. And, as such, in a position to make an informed guess about some of their activities.'

'And how would my...guess help you?'

Daya looked out of the window. The silence and sunshine seemed to amplify his fever, from which his thoughts emerged with dreamlike lucidity.

'I'm working on the assumption that the police did not kill Ghandy merely because he was a Maoist. Murmu, I believe, was *not* one. Therefore there was some other motive for their murder...I want to find out what it is.'

'Isn't that unnecessarily complicated?'

'How do you look at it?' Daya asked.

'As another unhappy episode in the so-called war against Maoism, a war in which no rules apply and to which every constitutional principle is sacrificed.'

'There may be other reasons, more immediate ones, more personal and uglier, if that is possible.'

'You mean in Murmu's case?'

'Perhaps. Was he connected to the party?'

Sudhir Pathak considered briefly. 'I don't think

so. In any case, these are hypothetical questions. The identity of the killers is not in doubt.'

'Not the actual killer, no. But I'm talking about those who gave him his orders. Do you really believe that the station officer acted alone?'

The tea arrived: it was black and bitter as Sudhir Pathak had promised. So far, thought Daya, he had failed to break down the man's granitic reserve.

'You take your job seriously,' Pathak observed.

'No more than the next man, I hope. Can you tell me how the party works?'

'The police would know.'

'I'm asking you.'

'Well, I can tell you what I know, there's nothing secret about it. The party was created some years ago when two separate groups with a history of mutual tension and disagreements decided to merge. Now there is a single command – a central committee, regional committees and, on the ground, operational commands. Ghandy was a member of the regional committee.'

'Did he work in the plateau?'

'Perhaps.'

'Why hasn't the party prohibited mining?'

'I doubt if it could. This isn't like Bastar, not what they call a liberated zone. It's an active theatre of war. If they tried there would be… repercussions. Besides, many villagers work as contractors or subcontractors for the company.'

Daya's fever was making him alternately cold and parched. He asked for a glass of water.

'I've heard that the company pays money to the Maoists?'

'The party levies what it calls a revolutionary tax – that is widely known.'

'So it's unlikely that the encounter could have been on the company's say-so?'

'Very unlikely.'

'And if it was of the usual kind,' Daya went on, pursuing his train of thought. 'In other words, a question of eliminating a Maoist or two, why call us in?'

'As to that, there could be many reasons,' Sudhir Pathak said amiably. 'The outcry in the press, factional considerations – the home minister is trying to supplant his boss, the chief minister. The latter takes a dim view of the situation and would like nothing better than to embarrass him. Besides, I don't think anybody expects your investigation to be particularly fruitful.'

'That sounds plausible,' admitted Daya. His fever was ebbing. Glancing out of the window, he saw his taxi pull up at the gate.

Sudhir Pathak hesitated. 'I can give you a couple of names,' he said finally. 'These are not people known to me personally, you understand. But I'm told they are knowledgeable. No doubt the police keep an eye on them…'

He wrote the names down on a piece of paper. 'They live in Sirkhedi.'

'Thank you,' Daya said, rising to his feet. 'I'll contact you again if I may, in case I need more information.'

'If you like,' said Pathak courteously. 'But I've told you all I know. In any case, I wish you luck.'

~

'What d'you mean you don't know where he is?'

'Just that...he left Sirkhedi a couple of days ago and no one has seen him since. He might be anywhere.'

'What about our man?'

'In a blue funk...he says the southerner made it clear he wasn't buying the story. But he won't find anything, he says.'

'I like that! I've already had Rajshekhar on the phone. He thinks the southerner is bad news. But he would, with the troubles he's having. Anyway, he's jumpy.'

'Why doesn't the minister speak to someone?'

'Think I haven't tried that? And they send *him* down. No, things are more complicated than that.'

'Maybe he's just trying to push up his price.'

'No, he's honest, and, what's worse, clever. At least, that's what they say. Where's my phone? ... Yes, it's me. Listen, about that inspector, the southerner, yes, him – what's his name? Dayanidhi – yes, he's beginning to make a nuisance of himself...I'm worried, the minister is worried too.

You know what Rajshekhar's done for us…no, of course I don't mean that, he'll work behind the scenes, he doesn't expect to be nominated… If it wasn't for the agency, I'd deal with it myself, but in things like that we defer to you…the minister told me that yesterday – how highly he thinks of you, how glad he is to help. Surely the encounter isn't important; two Maoists less to worry about, why would anyone have a problem with that? Which is why I can't make out… Yes, I agree, that's water under the bridge now…no, he's not the kind to talk, but still… All right, I'm relying on you.'

~

After a day's rest Daya felt well enough to take a walk. It was a quiet neighbourhood with a smattering of colonial houses: they evoked a bland, bucolic vision of bungalows with red roofs, a silver lake, yellow fields, the statuary of trees – neem and anjan, others whose names he had forgotten – bathing unhappy days in a retrospective glow.

He rang Sudha K. to find out where Murmu's parents lived and whether he would need an interpreter to talk to them.

'It might be a good idea.'

'Could you suggest someone?'

'I can ask Kemat to go with you if you like. He's related to the family in some obscure way.'

Daya gratefully accepted the offer. It was agreed that Kemat would meet him at the bus station the next morning. While waiting for their bus to depart he learned something about his companion. Like Murmu, Kemat hailed from the plateau. His ambition, he confided to Daya, was to become a journalist.

Kemat had a large pockmarked face with a cheerful expression: even his immobile eye seemed to derive an ironic pleasure from life. The air of an epicurean, someone with a talent for finding consolation in any situation. One of his cousins had joined the Maoists, another was a priest. According to him, priests were great hypocrites in the matter of women. Daya dozed off with the word 'women' ringing opulently in his ears.

They reached their destination in the afternoon (the bus having been delayed by various unforeseen but more or less expected contingencies), and disembarked where a dirt road branched from the highway. At the turning stood a concrete building which Kemat identified as a convent.

'D'you think we'll be able to catch a bus to Sirkhedi afterwards?' asked Daya. He was feeling tired and sleepy, a bit unwell.

'It might be difficult.'

'Perhaps we should stay the night here in that case.'

Kemat looked doubtful. 'I suppose you could ask the headman…I can stay with Murmu's family.'

'Would they put me up?'

'Of course.'

'I'd prefer that.'

Pointing to the convent, Kemat said: 'I have a cousin there…we'd get some tea,' he ended wistfully.

Daya laughed and clapped him on the shoulder. 'Let's go.'

So they had tea with two pretty nuns in the convent's reception room. It was furnished with shiny sofas, a table with a vase of plastic flowers, and, on the wall, a lithograph of the crucified Christ. As they walked down the dirt road that led to the village, its inhabitants, returning from work, studied them with covert curiosity.

Murmu's family lived in a brick-walled hut at the outskirts of the settlement. The overhang of the roof made a verandah where they sat waiting for his father. He arrived when it was almost dark, a short, middle-aged man with opaque eyes. They followed him into a large room lit by a single electric bulb flickering fitfully. A bamboo partition enclosed the kitchen: the glow of a fire was visible through the chinks. The room was furnished with string cots and some iron chests and cupboards pushed against the wall. In one corner stood cylindrical containers taller than a man, made of bamboo plastered with mud – storage bins for rice, Kemat explained. Sickles, a fishing net and an axe hung from pegs in the wall. Corncobs were suspended from the rafters. There was an open loft piled high with objects, its slats blackened with smoke.

Daya counted three children: a boy, an older girl, a baby in a hammock. A young man entered and ducked his head in greeting. Murmu's father sat at the edge of the cot, hands dangling between his knees. The dim light made it hard to read his expression. Daya learned that the household consisted of him and his wife, a grown-up son and *his* wife (the baby in the hammock was theirs), and two younger children. Had Stephen been the oldest then? No, there was one more: a daughter who had taken holy orders. Five children then, not counting those dead in infancy.

Stephen had studied here in the village for a few years before his father took him out to enrol in a mission school. After graduating, he went to college in the plains. From the age of eight he'd lived in hostels and rented rooms, coming home only in the holidays or when he fell ill (he had suffered from malaria). Some of this was related by his mother who came out of the kitchen – she had a small, round face and a voice like running water. The son sat in a corner whittling a stick. The boy had disappeared; his sister was playing with the baby.

One day Stephen had brought home a girl, the sister of one of his friends, saying they'd fixed things up. His father paid the bride price by selling a cow. She stayed with them until Stephen graduated and began practising in Sirkhedi. They came home when they could, at festivals and Christmastime. He bought a motorcycle and applied for a loan to build a house.

'What about the Maoists?'

Stephen hadn't been a Maoist, his father said wearily. Nor had he spoken all that much about them. Hereabouts the party was a fact of life – like the police. He knew people who had gone underground – perhaps he had even maintained contact with some of them for his own protection…

His father went to meet him after he was arrested. Stephen asked him to arrange money for a lawyer. Later he became more worried and uneasy – once he'd shown them marks of torture, stealthily, for a guard was always present. Yet a beating (or worse) was one of the hazards of being arrested: more worrying were the charges floating like chaff in the air. Even to visit him in jail was a difficult business – the journey took four hours and sometimes they were turned away without explanation.

Still, things could be worse: at least a trial would be held, there was a good chance of acquittal. Or so they thought – until one evening someone rang up to say that Stephen had been killed. Messengers carried the news to relatives, who began arriving during the night. At dawn, about twenty people set out for Sirkhedi on foot. Two hours later they were squatting in front of the police station, guarded by a ring of armed men. They waited silently (except for the ritual keening of women) all through the day and the next night with that stubborn tenacity which outlives anger or hope. In the morning some local businessmen, joined by the honourable member for Sirkhedi, tried to persuade them to go home – the delay was procedural, an autopsy had to be performed. That evening they were handed Stephen's remains without further explanation. Messengers fanned out again, and when all those who needed to be present had arrived, the ashes were interred.

'Why do you think they killed him?' asked Daya.

There was silence. To these men and women, Daya realized with a sudden shock, justice and the rule of law were inconceivable as abstractions, principles of state. They had never known them, they had only experienced the arbitrary exercise of power. The silence was broken by Stephen's brother – so far he had not spoken at all.

'They thought he was a troublemaker.'

Kemat began a low-voiced colloquy with him. Daya leaned back in his chair exhausted – by the journey, his illness, the strain of following an unknown language for nuance and inflection. He had almost dozed off when Kemat hesitantly touched his wrist: their host was asking if they would like to drink some rice beer.

'I've heard of it,' said Daya. 'Yes, why not?'

Kemat's face lit up with delight: he wanted a drink badly and had been afraid the inspector would refuse. To conceal his relief he began a long disquisition on the virtues of rice beer, which ended only when Murmu's mother came up to them carrying a large earthenware bowl. She held it out to Daya, who cupped it with both hands; to his surprise she put her own hands lightly over his. 'Now you must drink,' Kemat whispered in his ear, and Daya obediently lifted the bowl to his mouth and drank a draught of the cool, slightly bitter liquid. The old woman kept her hands like that, covering his, until he lowered the bowl. Then, dropping them, she inclined her body in a slight bow and turned away.

'That's the traditional way of welcoming a guest,' Kemat explained. He went through the ceremony in turn, sitting on the floor rather than his chair. When it was over he scrambled up again and plunged his face into the bowl like a child.

The rice beer proved to be all that Kemat had promised and more. After finishing it Daya felt light-headed and happy. He looked around the hut: the children had eaten and lay sleeping in a corner huddled in blankets.

They ate sitting on the ground out of brass plates; the fare was rice and a fowl cooked in tamarind sauce – so Kemat said, grunting with satiety. Meanwhile beds were being prepared for them. Kemat was still chatting with their host when Daya fell asleep. He awoke in the morning feeling refreshed but stiff: the cot was small and he had been obliged to sleep with legs folded. He asked for the bathroom and was taken to a roofless enclosure with walls of wattle and daub. He had washed and brushed his teeth by the time Kemat emerged from the hut, yawning noisily.

After they had drunk tea, the old man showed them the family chapel, a narrow lean-to embellished with a plaster statue of the Virgin with the infant Jesus in her lap. The base was sculpted to resemble rocks, and a plaster crucifix hung on the wall. It had been built with money sent by their daughter, the nun. Kemat lit a candle. When they came out Daya asked if it was possible to meet Murmu's widow.

In that case they should hurry, said Kemat – the best time to find people was early in the morning. He went in search of a car to hire, returning to say that its owner was asking for too much money. 'It's all right,' said Daya hastily, anxious to be off. They bade goodbye to their hosts. Daya walked to the turn-off, leaving Kemat to complete the transaction. In a few minutes the car roared up.

The morning was clear and gelid, an unbroken eggshell upon which birds tapped with sharp fluting calls. Once the sun emerged it would harden into a shimmering mosaic, an infinite set of variations on only a few colours: green, brown, yellow, blue. But in the meantime it resembled a delicate tapestry against which birds rose and dipped like indecipherable runes.

They found the widow at home. She had a dark face, a beauty difficult to pin down, so subtle and fine were its indications. Her brother watched uneasily as they talked to her, children crowding the doorway. She spoke haltingly, mostly in dialect. Daya led her through the events after Murmu's death, hoping in that way to put her at ease.

'What did you know about your husband's work?' he asked.

'Something.'

'Was he in touch with the party?'

'Occasionally he'd get a message about cases he appeared in.'

'And the party didn't object to his...other activities?'

'Not that I know of.'

'Was he worried about anything?'

'He was worried about me! I'd had a miscarriage – he wanted me to go to my parents' house to rest if I got pregnant again.'

'Anything else? Any threats?'

'Just suggestions to lay off or he'd get into trouble.'

'From the police?'

'Not just the police. Others as well – townspeople, colleagues.'

'And what was his reaction?'

'He tried to be careful. In any case, he didn't work alone.'

'What kind of man was your husband?' Daya asked.

She looked puzzled.

'I mean in his habits, temperament.'

'He was a good man – he worked hard, worried about his family. People would come to him for help and he'd try to help them. It irritated me sometimes, that and the amount of travelling he did – it was as though he had an itch in his feet.'

'Any enmities?'

She shook her head vigorously. 'Nothing. There were people who didn't like him, but no quarrels over land or money, nothing like that. He didn't drink – or very little…'

'What did you think about his work?'

She looked down at her hands.

'He should have minded his own business,' her brother interrupted sombrely.

When they were back in the car, Daya asked, 'Do you think she'll marry again?'

'Why not? She's young, pretty, childless…I've heard that she was having an affair,' Kemat added almost apologetically.

Daya showed no surprise. Instead he asked, 'Did you know Murmu personally?'

'Not well.'

'What did you make of him?'

'It's hard to say. He liked making speeches. Yet he wasn't ambitious in the usual sense…I think he liked being a lawyer. And he could be critical of the party.'

'Did he worry about the risk?'

'Well, he occupied an unusual position. Partly because of his legal work. Because of it the party left him alone. For him, there was no risk from the Maoists – who can be dangerous too, under certain circumstances. The only risk was from the police…'

'I was told that new leases have been granted. Who owns them?'

'Companies, consortia…Murmu was trying to get details: I think he'd filed an application in the commissioner's office.'

'I see,' Daya said thoughtfully.

~

The mansion in which the head priest lived was liberally garnished with cornices and plaster statutes. It stood in the centre of a warren of buildings – shops, living quarters, a Vedic school. At the door Daya was told that the time for audiences was later in the day. He gave the man his card and asked him to take it inside.

The antechamber was floored in marble, cladded too, to half the height of the walls. After a few minutes the attendant returned. He led Daya through a narrow corridor into a large hall covered with carpets and cushions. At one end stood a gilt chair with smaller sofas flanking it. Daya sat down in one of them. A door opened and the godman walked in accompanied by a middle-aged couple. The man was fat and pursy, dressed in a safari suit, with gold-rimmed spectacles; the woman wore a silk sari. They took their leave by going down on their hands and knees and knocking their foreheads against the floor. The godman lifted his hand in benediction and turned to Daya as they backed away with folded hands, ducking their heads respectfully.

Daya explained that he had dropped in to pay his respects, qualifying the word with a vague, ambiguous gesture. 'I also wanted to obtain your opinion of the case I'm investigating – as a respected figure, a public-spirited citizen,' he ended amiably.

The godman nodded – he was bald and black-bearded, with a formidable belly, dressed in a dhoti, a shawl thrown around his shoulders against the cold.

'As a monk, a man of God, I can only say that everything seems crystal clear. I very much regret that the station officer is being subjected to this… persecution.' His voice was oddly light and fluting.

'I'm afraid I don't follow,' Daya said politely.

'I was referring to your inquiry. Not that I doubt your sincerity and good faith – I would never do that – but you must admit it smacks of vindictiveness.'

'Then I take it you regard the encounter as genuine?'

'Absolutely. The station officer is a God-fearing man, assiduous in maintaining order despite the wretched state of the countryside…so much of it is in the hands of those bandits.'

'So you condone the deaths?'

'Of course, since they were killed lawfully while trying to escape… Religion doesn't teach us to be merciful to evildoers: it exhorts us to punish them.'

'What is your opinion of the station officer?'

'He is – I will not say a friend – but a valued acquaintance, someone I would vouch for unhesitatingly. We sleep sounder at night because of him.'

'The disorder in the countryside doesn't seem to have affected your establishment, at any rate,' Daya remarked.

'It only looks that way… Even we [he shifted to the royal pronoun] have to take precautions, not that they would dare to touch *us.* Atheists, revolutionaries, but God will punish them…'

On that minatory note the audience concluded.

~

'What's he doing?' asked the dark man, gesturing indolently to a waiter. His companion, bald and long-faced, followed his gaze with anxiety.

'He hasn't seen you,' he said deferentially and raised a hand, snapping his fingers with a loud click. The waiter scurried over to them.

The dark man ordered a drink. 'Not him,' he said when the waiter had gone. 'I meant the southerner. What's *he* doing? Or does anybody know?' he added with heavy sarcasm.

They were sitting in a luxurious restaurant embellished with creamy marble, enormous chandeliers, stiff, heavy drapes, silver-plated cutlery. The air conditioning was icy cold, the silence deep and restful. Below them, through thick plate-glass windows, they could see cars scudding along the road like fish in an aquarium.

'He's back in Sirkhedi,' the bald man admitted.

'So I hear. We don't need more...complications. Things are delicately poised. As you know.'

'What do you mean?'

'No embarrassments, and, above all, no publicity.'

'Are you thinking of the opposition?'

The dark man sighed delicately in exasperation. 'Not the opposition, we've already sounded them out...if necessary we can offer a quid pro quo. No, it's publicity I'm worried about.'

'There's no need to worry,' the bald man said uncertainly.

'I don't like it. Particularly since no one seems to know what he's up to.'

'He won't find anything.'

'There's always something,' the dark man corrected. 'To find, I mean… Let's hope your man in Sirkhedi can keep a lid on things.'

'He's a blunt instrument,' the bald man admitted. 'But reliable. Besides he's in as deep as any of us.'

'He has less to lose.'

'Only his job,' the bald man said. His companion's insinuations were beginning to set his teeth on edge. Trying to change the subject he said, 'Another drink?'

'Well, it's your lookout,' said the dark man, pursuing his own train of thought. 'Yes, I'll have one.'

~

Daya had already met one of the men recommended by Pathak. From him he obtained a useful precis of the Maoist movement in the region. The man referred guardedly to factional tendencies in the party.

'You mean its leadership?' asked Daya.

'Yes.'

'What kind of differences?'

'It's hard to say. Some are over tactical questions – where to expand and how fast, whether to build urban bases, contradictions between local concerns and wider issues.'

More than that he did not know or would not say.

Daya arranged to meet the second man in an eatery outside town. 'On the basis of hearsay I can tell you what I know,' he said finally. 'I assume you're aware of the arrangement with the company?'

Daya nodded.

'It is an old one... A minority objected to it, the majority supported it on pragmatic grounds. Then talk of new leases began to spread, and that reopened the question. Of how to respond to them, I mean. There was a debate which ended inconclusively.'

'Did Ghandy take part in it?'

'Undoubtedly.'

'And what was his position – purely as a guess?'

The man hesitated. 'Let's say that he was something of an idealist.'

'What about the attack on the company's depot? Was it made to persuade it to accept an... enhanced tax?'

'Perhaps.'

Daya looked down thoughtfully at his fly-specked cup. Outside a dog barked and scratched its ear. A motorcycle roared past, raising a cloud of dust.

~

When Daya announced his intention of questioning the policemen who had been in Kakrana that day, the station officer proved surprisingly cooperative. He rang up to say that they had been ordered to present themselves before him, all except three – one was sick and two had gone on leave. He would let the inspector know when they returned.

Daya questioned the men patiently and meticulously. As he had expected, M'ta and the sergeant stuck to their story. The third man was on vacation. The others had nothing much to say – they had only carried the bodies up, after all. When Daya asked them about their work, they complained of bad housing and the endless hours spent on duty. None of them was from the district and they displayed the usual mixture of contempt and prejudice towards its inhabitants. They spoke of the Maoists with respect and fear as strange, uncanny adversaries, the more uncanny for being ragged and badly armed.

In the evening Daya found an envelope on the floor of his room. In it was a piece of paper torn from a notebook with a name and address. The writing was large and laborious. The caretaker said that someone had come with it while he was out.

Daya returned to the capital, where Kemat was waiting for him. He cheerfully undertook to deliver a summons to Jagdish Khartiya: constable, police precinct, Sirkhedi, currently on leave. Kemat estimated that he could return with Khartiya the next day – if he obeyed the summons.

'He'll obey,' Daya said. 'The question is whether he'll "get advice" before coming. That's what we need to prevent at all costs.'

And he told Kemat what to say.

After Kemat had left, he went over the case in his mind obsessively, fruitlessly, like a dog chasing its own tail. He remembered another fictional detective who had compared the hounds of law with the hounds of the lord. Meaning the Dominicans. There were times when it seemed to Daya that he had met Captain Bellodi in person, drunk a cup of coffee with him. Other figures seemed just as familiar – Levin, for example, or Julien Sorel. Dorothea (did she have a second name or had he forgotten it?).

The Dominicans… Daya had studied in a

Catholic school run by the Salesians. His only consolation at the time was reading – he would spend every break in the library, buried in a book. When school ended, he had to wait, sometimes for quite a long time, for the rickshaw that brought his sister from her school before picking him up. The library was closed and he would walk gingerly through the empty, echoing corridors with their green dado, peering into classrooms where the smell of chalk and dust still lingered. Sometimes he'd run into a priest (there were living quarters at the back of the school) who would look at him quizzically and pass briskly on. Not all of them wore a soutane, which confused him: in his mind the two had become indivisible. As the years passed, his memory endowed these images – receding stone-flagged corridors, playing grounds without a blade of grass, rows of trees through which the afternoon sun shone – with a tinge of melancholy as impalpable as the dust.

One of his teachers had been a priest – despite his name, Father Bartholomew came from Goa.

He taught English to the senior classes. In class he would declaim poems from the textbook in a mellifluous voice, with feeling, one hand clutching the buttons of his soutane. Tennyson ('The Charge of the Light Brigade'), Robert Frost ('The Road not Taken'), Hopkins ('Margaret, are you grieving / Over Goldengrove unleaving' and 'This darksome burn, horseback brown / His rollrock highroad rolling down')… The boys in front would stare at him uncomprehendingly while those in the back sniggered. He kept order by the force of his somewhat theatrical personality, stalking up and down the rows, never speaking any language but English, paying attention only to those who were good at it – their questions he answered clearly and patiently.

Twenty years later, when Daya went to visit him, he was miraculously unchanged, his face smooth and unlined, his hair black and shiny. A valetudinarian, he boasted of his ill-health, spoke darkly of attempts to prevent him from becoming principal. He complained of the post's difficulties

– the bureaucratic grind, the faculty's bickering, their laziness and insensitivity, the resistance to reform. Yet, despite his complaints, Daya got the impression that he was happy.

For the first time Daya noticed what a terrible snob he was: proud of his background, proud of the fact that his ancestors had been Brahmins who rode in procession on an elephant and sat on a wooden throne. These glories had dwindled to a flat in Bombay where his mother lived; his brothers had emigrated to America. He confessed that he had no time to read now or even to teach – his administrative duties were too onerous.

~

That evening Daya phoned his sister.

'How is it going?' he asked, after they had greeted each other absently.

'All right, I suppose.'

'I know, but how is *she* feeling?' '*She*' was their mother, being treated for cancer.

'Much the same, I would say.' There was an undercurrent of hostility in his sister's voice.

'I'll come next month,' he promised.

'I think you should.'

'Has she been asking for me?'

'She asks sometimes but never complains – you know how she is. I told her you were busy.'

'I've been travelling, you know how it is… You sound tired.'

'I manage – there are people around all the time.' And she gave a concise account of relatives who had come to help.

'That's good,' he said, thinking how little he did by comparison. Well, he had better speak to her at least. 'Is she awake?'

His sister went to check and returned to say that no, she had dozed off. Daya felt relieved; he found it increasingly difficult to talk to his mother. With his father it had been even worse – he doubted if they had ever expressed their thoughts openly to each other except in moments of antagonism, irritation. Yet Daya did not in the least regret his childhood or feel impelled to psychoanalyse it. It had been perfectly normal and unremarkable, a bit lonely, spent in books and daydreams. Some children fail to develop a protective carapace – too much exposed, they withdraw into themselves for protection.

He remembered how his first girlfriend had said to him, seriously, a bit critically, 'You don't talk about your family *at all*,' and how he'd been taken aback by that even though it was true. He had been happy in Bangalore, where he went to university, back in the days when the city was still unchanged. He remembered an old disused temple of grey stone, like lava petrified into sweeping, flowing shapes. The urgent, cascading notes of the koel waking him early in summer. His friend Binda announcing exuberantly that he intended to be a writer. Binda was the first person he knew who also loved books, reading – from very early on his vocation was clear. He was what the French call a committed writer, *engagé*, but they rarely spoke of politics.

Daya studied history and then law. He sat for the civil services exam unwillingly, with no expectation of passing, and, contrary to all expectation, passed. Binda had been concerned when Daya told him. 'Are you sure you know what you're getting into?' he asked.

'Well, there's nothing in particular that I want to do. Unlike you…I doubt if I'd make a good lawyer, and being a manager in some firm doesn't appeal to me either. This way at least I get to do something useful.'

'You think,' Binda said darkly.

Nellie was more impressed, if only because he had shown some practical ability at last. On the other hand, she didn't much like the associations conjured by the term 'police' and wondered what kind of life it entailed.

'Don't worry,' Daya said. 'It'll probably be as desk-bound as any other job.'

Nellie was from the coast, with clear, glossy skin and a fund of cheerfulness and energy. She was uncertainly shedding her faith. Binda liked to discuss faith in philosophical terms – a background of devotional songs, myths and bedtime stories exerted a subliminal influence on him. Daya, on the other hand, was bored by it.

'You know,' Nellie announced one day. 'I don't think I could marry someone of a different religion. I used to think maybe I could, but not any longer.'

'Well, that rules me out then…'

Nellie was upset because he had made a joke about it ('as usual'), but then they had never discussed marriage seriously. She was the first girl he had gone to bed with; the softness of her skin was intoxicating and every metaphor he'd read about bodies and fruit became instantly real – fruit to be admired, plucked, eaten, with delight, without guilt.

He wondered what she thought of religion now, whether she'd taken to churchgoing. Maybe she lived in Dubai or San Francisco, in any case he hoped that she was happy. Her features had become a bit blurred, a bit distant, though he could remember the shape of her body as well as ever.

~

In the morning, a little after ten, someone knocked on the door: he opened it to find Kemat standing outside with Jagdish Khartiya. After shaking hands with them he took Kemat aside. Khartiya remained in the doorway looking nervously around him.

Kemat took his leave and the inspector ushered Khartiya inside. He was short and dark, with a broad, slightly aquiline nose, thick lips, round cheeks, hair brushed across his forehead. His body was short and solid, long-armed, thick-thighed: in short, an archetypal peasant lad, healthy, bright-eyed, handsome. Daya set about trying to put him at ease: How long had the journey taken? Had it been comfortable? What were the buses like? 'Would you like some tea?' he broke off to ask. Khartiya made an irresolute gesture signifying no, but Daya ignored it. 'Let's go to the canteen,' he said.

They went to the canteen. Daya chose a table near the window.

'How long is it since you joined the police?' he asked abruptly.

'Three years.'

'How old are you?'

'Twenty-five.'

'Why did you become a policeman?'

'I read a recruiting poster, applied, got selected.'

'I see…I expect you were good at sports.'

A flash of pride crossed Khartiya's face. 'I was the best runner in the district.'

'That must have helped in the physical exam,' Daya remarked. 'What about the rest?'

'I didn't have to pay, if that's what you mean,' Khartiya said. After a pause, he added: 'My uncle knew someone…'

'That always helps. What does your father do?'

'He's a farmer.'

'And you're the oldest son?'

'No, I have an elder brother, he's at home.'

'I suppose they're pleased with you – a government job, that's the best kind. Government "bread" is reliable. Once you're in, you're in for life – that's what they say, don't they? And it's true. Only sometimes there's an exception that proves the rule...'

Khartiya said nothing.

'Your boss, the station officer, is very close to losing his job,' Daya continued. 'I assume you know why... When did you join the special squad?'

'They picked us out during training. Technically speaking, I suppose we volunteered. I didn't mind at the time, no one did, it seemed more...' His voice trailed off uncertainly.

'Glamorous,' Daya finished. 'Yes, I can see that. And then?'

'We were put through more training: using semi-automatic weapons and knives, looking for landmines, things like that.'

'Where were you posted afterwards?'

'In Badalpur for a while, and after that, Sirkhedi.'

'How did your duties strike you?'

Khartiya said nothing.

'You can tell me – I'm a policeman too, remember? Working men over on suspicion of sheltering Maoists: not that they can help it, poor sods, the Maoists have guns too. And for others, the full treatment: electric shocks, the plastic bag, the bastinado. You're not supposed to need training for that – it's a matter of watching and learning. Nowadays they're called advanced interrogation techniques…'

'So?' Khartiya said, a trifle defiantly.

'The problem – provided you think of it as a problem – is that people get used to it. To treating men like animals. To impunity…so you take a pair of wires, attach one end to a car battery, the other to a man's balls, and watch him thrash like a fish out of water. The man howls – like an animal. His back arches, his mind empties. Think of it, try to imagine it…with a plastic bag over your head, what would happen to your lungs, your blood. But the worst is the interval: terror of the next spasm, the next bout of agony…and shame, of course. No wonder he confesses: in his place you'd do the same. But the paradox is that torture can only reduce a man to this level, an animal's level. Other things might do it too: sickness or hunger, for example. On the other hand, I've often wondered what happens to the torturer, what he becomes – in the psychological sense, here and now…'

Daya pushed his cup aside. 'What do you think of your boss?' he asked in the same quiet, even tone.

'He's a devil,' Khartiya said promptly, without thinking. A flash of fear crossed his face.

'A devil,' Daya repeated. 'Because he's a torturer and takes pleasure in it?'

'That too…'

'What else?'

'Nothing.'

'What kind of devil is he? What does he do?'

'It's private,' Khartiya said in a stifled voice.

'Is it something he did to you?'

Khartiya started to shake his head, then stopped. His eyes had become bloodshot with distress. Clearly, he was at the end of his tether.

'He's a devil,' he said finally. 'A devil who strips men of their dignity, even his own men.'

This obscure allusion – and it was clear that Khartiya would say no more – might have escaped Daya if he had not been immersed in recalling his schooldays. A memory stirred of certain youthful experiments. He paused before speaking, conscious that a misplaced word might snap the tenuous thread of trust between them.

'You mean that there are certain things that boys, young men, might do with each other, for pleasure, as an experiment, that become degrading, unspeakable when a stranger forces one to do them… Is that what you mean?'

Khartiya's face dissolved into a mask of unhappiness. So that's his secret, Daya thought. He recalled the faint sneer with which one of the men he had questioned had said apropos the station officer, 'Of course, he has his *favourites*.'

Then he recalled the station officer's physiognomy and Mandelstam's line about Stalin's cockroach whiskers.

'So you became his *favourite*... Were there others?'

'I don't think so.'

'I suppose that's why he selected you to accompany him. When did you realize what was going to happen?'

'Before we left – he told us.' Khartiya could no longer tell what upset him more – the sexual acts he had been forced to perform or the encounter. They had melted into a single hallucination in which he remained perpetually trapped.

'Where?'

'In his office. "We're going to get rid of them today," he said. We nodded. "Do you understand?" he asked again. "Those are orders from above." Later on he joked about accidents – it was a hint.'

'Who was with you?'

'Surab M'ta.'

'Is he a friend of yours?'

'You could say that.'

'Any others?'

Khartiya hesitated. 'One,' he said finally.

'What's his name?'

'Jairam Awasiya.'

'Tell me what happened.'

'The commandant ordered a halt, to rest. That was the signal. The men stood eyeing us. I could smell their sweat. "Sit to one side," the commandant ordered. He wanted them to walk towards the hill. It was bathed in sunshine. Where we were standing seemed dark by comparison. They stayed where they were. The commandant ordered them to move away again. "They're going to kill us," one of them said, I think it was Murmu. The other man didn't say anything. The sergeant cursed. "We don't like your smell, that's all," he said. He grabbed his shoulder and tried to wrench him around… Murmu just looked at us, turned around and started walking. The other man hurried to catch up with him. They had gone maybe six or seven paces when the sergeant fired…'

There was a pause.

'It's strange,' Khartiya continued haltingly. 'M'ta didn't shoot – he told me later that it was as though he'd been paralysed, he's still ashamed of it. Whereas I…I fired: it was reflex, I guess. I shot the man in front of me. That was all – the sound of shots, the men falling as though a puff of wind had knocked them down… The commandant went up to the bodies and poked them with his boot. Then he told us to drag them further away. After that we fired a few bursts into the grove and waited for the rest to come up.'

'How did they take it?'

'They knew what had happened.'

'Why were you sent on leave?'

'I felt tired and sick, had difficulty sleeping. The commandant said a break would do me good, help me pull myself together.'

'He thought you were squeamish.'

'It's part of the job after all.'

'What is?'

'Making sure criminals don't walk away.'

'No, it isn't, and not even if they're criminals. Did you watch Murmu's interrogation?'

Khartiya said nothing.

'You see…no questions, only exhortations to confess. When that happens you can be sure that you're settling other people's scores. Ever thought about it?'

'No.'

'What worries you then?'

'I don't know.'

'You wish the station officer had chosen someone else… Even if he had, it wouldn't have made much difference. In the long run, I mean. Did you know Murmu, had you run into him – before that day, I mean?'

'Yes,' Khartiya said evasively.

'How?'

'We were told to keep an eye on him.'

'Follow him around, you mean?'

'See what he was up to.'

'And did he know?'

'After a while, yes...that was the idea.'

'To intimidate him, you mean. And what impression did you get?'

Khartiya hesitated. 'He seemed harmless enough. Quite soon it became...routine. Sometimes when I was hanging around his house he'd call me over for a cup of tea.'

'Did you see his wife?'

Kharitya looked down. 'Yes,' he mumbled.

'Pretty, isn't she?'

'I guess so.'

'Let's go back a bit...the station officer told you that the order to kill them came from above?'

'Yes.'

'What kind of friends does he have?'

'Lots.'

'Ever hear him talk about mining?'

'Sometimes.'

'With whom?'

'Someone called Binoy Patnaik. I was on guard duty at his house when the phone rang. I took it to him, that's how I noticed the name. By then we were already keeping an eye on Murmu.'

'How often did he speak to Patnaik?'

'I don't know but I got the impression that he knew him well.'

Daya looked at his watch. 'Let's eat something,' he said briskly.

Later, he took Khartiya to his room, where he made out a deposition. 'Here,' he said, handing it to him.

'I can't sign,' Khartiya muttered. 'I'll lose my job.'

'You'll have to turn approver, yes. I'll do my best to protect you, which means keeping this confidential until I find more evidence. But losing your job is hardly the worst thing that could happen. Now that you know what it can entail...'

Khartiya listened gloomily. 'I'll think it over,' he said.

'Of course. Keep this...I'll write down my address and phone number. You can send it to me when you decide to sign.'

He made a copy for himself while Khartiya stared out of the window.

~

Daya found a service directory in the reading room, and riffled the pages in search of a familiar name. After a while he found one: Tariq Qureishi – they had been in training school together. According to Daya's unreliable memory of those far-off, far from golden years, he had been a probationer of average ability and ambition. He rang the number.

Tariq placed him straight away. 'When shall we meet?' he said effusively. 'I'm there on Friday for an official briefing. They go on forever – quite pointless, of course.'

They agreed to meet for lunch. On Saturday Daya made his way to the Eastern Provinces Club – founded 1890, according to a sign over the doorway. He was directed to the bar, where Tariq was waiting.

'You've changed,' was his first comment. 'Not too much, but still; you're already going grey, you should dye your hair. Whereas me, I look much the same… Let's order drinks; meanwhile tell me about yourself, what you've been up to, how you joined the agency, why you haven't attended a single reunion of the class up until now – you haven't, have you?'

'No,' Daya admitted.

'Why on earth not?'

'Too clubby…'

Tariq laughed and said, 'No, you haven't changed.'

They ordered drinks. Tariq pulled a wry face when he learned that Daya wasn't married. He'd been married eight years – no seven-year itch yet, he joked – and had two children. Carried away on the tide of his garrulity, Daya gave him a synopsis of his own career. Though they had joined the service at the same time, Tariq outranked him. 'Therefore it's been quite unremarkable, as you can see,' he concluded.

'But what's it like to work in the agency? You get the important cases, the hot potatoes.'

'Sometimes.'

'What are you doing here? Is it the Kakrana affair?'

'Yes.'

'A sticky case,' Tariq said with a grimace. By *sticky* he meant thankless, troublesome. 'I won't ask what you make of it...fortunately I haven't been posted to a disturbed district yet. Junior officers get out of hand there: it's the devil to control them. If something goes wrong, you're forced to cover up to protect your own record. And, of course, there's no shortage of people telling you that results can't be obtained by following procedures. Procedures, that's a laugh! How on earth do you convince a constable that beating a man to pulp isn't the only – or even the best – way of obtaining proof?... I tell you, it can't be done.'

The conversation turned to Tariq's current assignment. The secret, he confided, was to avoid any suggestion of the new broom or delve too deeply into his subordinates' methods: no, best to curtail the most flagrant abuses indirectly, through well-placed warnings. Within these limits he did his job conscientiously, by the book.

After lunch they went to the terrace to smoke.

'What do you know about Binoy Patnaik?' Daya asked.

'A fixer,' Tariq replied promptly. 'High up, politically well connected. Why?'

'His name cropped up in connection with something… Is there anyone he's particularly close to?'

'You know how it works – you keep your bases covered, what goes down comes around, and so on. Of late he's said to be close to Reddy. Reddy is our home minister – technically my boss, though I've had very little to do with him fortunately. That doesn't make him happy, he wants to be chief minister. And, as you can imagine, that doesn't make the chief minister happy. Both of them are busy pulling wires in Delhi. So far it's a stalemate.'

'Didn't Reddy return to the party recently?'

'And was welcomed with open arms. The chief minister's faction doesn't care for him. He's a wily bird – doesn't play for peanuts if you know what I mean.'

'I see.'

'I hope you're not after him,' Tariq said perceptively. 'He's a big fish, too big. The idea is preposterous…just take my word for it.'

'I'm curious.'

'Remember the adage about the cat?'

'What adage?' asked Daya innocently.

~

Back at the institute, Daya went methodically through a pile of old newspapers and magazines until he had obtained a precis of Reddy's career. The minister was reported to be close to a pair of mining barons who belonged to the same caste. When taxed with their shenanigans, he replied that it was natural for his friends to throw their weight about while he was in office – what use was his friendship otherwise? This happy retort was often quoted as proof of his constancy (in return for which he demanded an equally unshakeable loyalty).

The chief minister, with whom Reddy had a running feud, was inordinately fond of appearing on television, and also of promoting his son's career (his son was a film producer). There was nothing unusual in this paternal solicitude, but it did detract from the business of government more than was thought suitable. Recently Reddy had objected to a government contract, citing accusations of corruption. The chief minister retorted that as member of the cabinet which approved the said contract, these doubts had taken a trifle long to surface. Reddy replied that the contract had not been adequately discussed. And so it went on.

Daya paid a visit to the department of mines and minerals. Confronted with his polite intransigence the initial effort at obstruction melted like snow. The relevant files were hastily brought out.

'How big are the concessions?' he asked. 'How much are they worth potentially?'

The secretary steepled his fingers. 'If the company is taken as a standard of comparison – by that I mean its annual output – then, according to our surveys, the first concession is bigger, the second comparable in size, the third smaller and more speculative.'

'How many bids were received?'

'Each concession had a slightly different set of criteria. Some companies bid for more than one… there were twelve bids in all.'

'And how were the winners selected?'

'According to the usual parameters. The royalty is fixed, so it was a matter of evaluating their technical expertise, size, solvency, experience, things like that…'

'The job doesn't appear to be complicated.'

'There's considerable outlay on infrastructure and processing; compensation, of course; environmental regulations, labour laws, the Maoists… It's not an easy environment to work in, by any means.'

'But no shortage of bidders...I'd like copies of the bid documents and contracts.'

'Sure,' the secretary said glumly.

'When are the leases supposed to become operational?'

'It's in the documents; there are penalty clauses as well.'

'Thank you,' said Daya, wondering how soon after his departure the secretary would pick up the phone – probably before he left the building.

Everything depended on Khartiya, his sense of unease and compunction. Whatever its roots, the feeling was rare, and because of it Daya felt a bond of sympathy with the younger man. Meanwhile he decided to go to Delhi to report on the progress of the case and make arrangements for various eventualities.

~

Delhi huddled under a grey blanket of fog which obscured and muffled, foreshortening the imperial perspectives of Lutyens' quarter. Its gardens glowed like jewels when the sun came out; its monuments loomed more insistently, visions of power and paranoia with almost nothing on a human scale or expressive of civic feeling.

Daya wrote out a brief report, omitting any mention of Reddy's name and asking for help in view of the inquiry's widening scope. His request was granted. A week later he had an assistant – a plump, taciturn man, a southerner like himself, whose name, for purposes of convenience, had been shortened to Venkat. Daya gave him his instructions; his deputy nodded and set to work.

Upon returning home Daya found a package from Binda containing a copy of his new novel, and an unmarked envelope with his address written in Hindi. In it was Khartiya's confession, duly signed. He laid it down with a feeling of elation mixed with concern, and immediately began considering the plans he had been making for this unlikely eventuality.

After drinking a cup of coffee he decided to

ring Binda up. His friend's number was busy. Daya was leafing through the novel when the phone rang. It was Kemat; the line was bad and Daya was barely able to make out the word 'suicide' amidst the crackle. 'Where?' he asked, dazed. 'So that's why he signed,' he thought, recalling Khartiya's face with its broad cheekbones and ashy pallor.

Automatically Daya picked up the envelope, phone still pressed to his ear. The postmark was smudged, the date illegible. Not that it mattered. Perhaps he had decided to kill himself before signing. Or perhaps he had posted the letter in a moment of desperation, then spent hours, days weighing up the consequences, working out the sum of possibilities, before deciding it came to this.

Kemat knew only the bare outlines – a constable had died after swallowing the contents of a bottle of pesticide. Of course, thought Daya bleakly, he wouldn't have a gun with him, not while on leave. The autopsy would be conducted at the district hospital. There was another thing – Stephen's widow had gotten in touch with him: somebody from Kakrana…Kemat's voice was fading; he added something about the police station being like an overturned anthill before the call ended.

Daya went to the director's office the next morning to obtain authorization for the station officer's arrest.

'We'll have to inform the police,' the director pointed out.

'Only at the end…meanwhile I'd like a warrant made out.'

'All right. But be careful, tread on eggshells – I want proof, not speculations.'

~

Daya set about defying that advice by calling up a journalist, an acquaintance of his. Since he had acquired a reputation for inaccessibility, for *not* leaking information or giving interviews, his call evoked interest. They arranged to meet at an eatery the journalist had discovered recently and swore by.

Over a glass of beer, Daya unfolded his reconstruction of the case.

'Interesting,' said the journalist when he had finished. 'But what do you want me to write?'

'Everything, as far as I'm concerned, but not now, later. The timing is vital.'

The journalist nodded. 'Fair enough. Did I tell you that I knew Ghandy? It was many years ago, when we were students but still... Today it seems incredible, I mean a man like that, with a promising career, chucking it away. Oh, I know it used to happen in the sixties, but that was then, this is now. Back then there were those who died, but others who sowed their wild oats and became pillars of respectability. Amongst academics of a certain age, a Naxalite past gives a certain *cachet*, material for an amusing article, a certain amount of self-promotion. It's true, I read one recently: it was far from amusing, or only in an infantile way. But Ghandy was serious and that's what makes it incredible...'

'The fact that he became a Maoist or that he was killed?'

The journalist drained his glass: 'Everything!'

'Frankly,' Daya said slowly, 'I'm interested in the other man, Murmu. After all, he had fewer ideals to justify the risks he ran… Besides, Ghandy could have walked away, whereas Murmu had nowhere to go. He was a marked man. Yes, he had the choice of keeping silent, but that's the whole point–'

'Whether you agree or not, it's what makes the story news – proof that Ghandy was killed in cold blood, as part of an organized conspiracy. Coupled with his background, it makes for an exposé; adds a touch of human interest if you know what I mean. Otherwise do you think anyone cares if – or even how – a Maoist gets killed?'

Daya knew what he meant, though he did not much care for the meaning: weasel words, lawyers' language. As for himself, he distrusted everything and everybody out of habit, an ingrained scepticism (which did not prevent him from holding political opinions).

Together they worked out what the journalist would write.

'Let's order,' the journalist said when they had finished. 'The seekh kebabs here are really incredible.'

~

It was a beautiful day. The unkempt garden with its bougainvillea and roses, crooked trees, patches of grass, tangles of shrubbery was alive with a gossamer web of sounds – bird calls, the chatter of squirrels, a child's voice, the muffled roar of a bus. They sharpened and faded, a muted aria perpetually reshuffling its elements. But Daya, immersed in his thoughts, barely noticed.

The door opened and the station officer entered. He looked around warily before taking a chair, explaining that he had been delayed by a call from headquarters.

'Shall we begin?' Daya asked frostily.

'Why not?'

'Your full name?'

A glint of repressed anger showed in the station

officer's eyes. Daya wrote his reply down.

'Let's begin with one of your men, the one who committed suicide.'

'Why?' the station officer demanded. 'What's he got to do with it?'

'Khartiya was present when the prisoners were shot, wasn't he?'

'So?'

'Now suddenly he kills himself. Why?'

'How should I know? He had personal problems.'

'What kind of problems?'

'Am I my brother's keeper? Debts, a love affair, a family quarrel – it could be anything.'

'Or maybe something to do with his job…'

'That's impossible.'

'Why?'

'I was his boss, I would know.'

'Maybe he kept his worries to himself. What kind of policeman was he?'

'A good one: he did his work well. I had no

complaints.'

'Why did you send him home?'

'He asked to go; he had leave owing, what was I supposed to do? Besides, I figured the rest would do him good – the job isn't easy, there's a lot of stress involved.'

'Things like the encounter, you mean… Did it upset him?'

'Why would he get upset over something like that?'

'Not even if Murmu and Ghandy were killed in cold blood?'

'Who says that?' the station officer demanded.

'Khartiya did.'

There was a pause.

'Does it worry you?' Daya asked. 'That he admitted to it?'

'Disturb me? No…besides, he couldn't have admitted to anything of the kind.'

'You did your best to keep me from questioning him. A clumsy, amateurish attempt: I'd have obtained his address anyway. As it turned out, I didn't need to. Did you ask his family if he'd gone anywhere? I can see you did... Well, he came to meet me.'

There was another pause.

'We had an illuminating conversation,' continued Daya. 'Shall I tell you about it?'

'If you insist.'

'It's my pleasure. He described the actual events of that day in detail, right from the time you indicated that the prisoners were to be killed. How, after reaching the bottom of the hill, they were shot in the back. He also told me of certain things you made him do, sexual acts that you forced upon him–'

'He lied!' the station officer interrupted violently.

'About what?'

The station officer controlled himself with an effort. 'I don't believe you,' he said stonily. 'But if he did say all that, he lied.'

'For what you made him do, the degradation

you subjected him to, there is nothing that can be done, unfortunately. Khartiya is dead…The sexual episodes filled him with shame and self-loathing; the murder you made him commit proved to be the final straw. But at least he acted under duress, in obedience to orders…'

'Nothing that Khartiya says – said rather – is proof.'

'Oh, I have something better than words. I have a signed deposition – would you like to see it?'

He handed the station officer a photocopy of Khartiya's confession.

'His suicide clinches it,' Daya said conversationally. 'If he had lived you'd have tried your best to make him retract – who knows, you might even have succeeded. But now there's not a judge who won't believe it…what do you think?'

The station officer licked his lips. The muscles of his face had gone slack. Restlessly he drummed one foot against the floor, then, becoming aware of the noise, stopped abruptly.

'Nothing…it's a pack of lies.'

'What reason would a dead man have for lying? No, for you this is the end: I have a warrant for your arrest in my pocket.'

'You can't arrest me,' the station officer said uncertainly.

'Why not? I won't prevent you from leaving the room, but I've every intention of arresting you as soon as the formalities are complete.'

'Why would I want to kill them?' The station officer was deflating visibly.

'Why indeed? I have an idea about that as well…a great deal of money has been invested here recently. Some people wanted to…protect their investments, shall we say? So Murmu was arrested as a warning, to get him to lay off. Shortly after, Ghandy dropped like a plum into your hands. With someone like that, knowing what you knew, an encounter was always on the cards. Only, your friends had the brilliant idea of killing two birds with one stone – but for that Murmu would have to be taken out of prison.' Daya tapped the deposition with a finger. 'I asked Khartiya,' he continued, 'if someone else was involved. Now I want you to think very carefully before answering. This confession implicates you beyond a shadow of doubt. However, if you can show that you acted under instructions, pressure from above, that would mitigate your culpability. Think it over.'

The station officer licked his lips. Judging that he had inspired the maximum of unease consistent with economy of information, Daya leaned back and said quietly, 'That is all for now.'

~

The station officer was arrested at dawn the next day. A small group of policemen from Badalpur witnessed the ceremony, seeming positively apologetic. The station officer, bleary-eyed and rumpled, made no protest. Evidently he'd spent a sleepless night. After a perfunctory search of his quarters, Daya sent him off to the guardhouse in Venkat's custody while he sped to Kakrana through a strong wind that rattled the panes of the car and unrolled the mist from the landscape.

At the village he found a deputation of peasants waiting for him. Daya explained that he had obtained evidence casting doubt upon the official version of events. On the basis of that evidence the station officer had been arrested – this very morning, in fact. A breath of incredulity seemed to pass through the gathering at the news.

He invited anybody with any knowledge of what had happened that day to speak. After a pause a middle-aged man got up: he had thick greying hair, a thick moustache, and a worried expression on his face. He spoke uncertainly at first, looking around him for reassurance, but gained fluency after a while. Daya could follow what he said without too much difficulty. The burden of his preliminary remarks – Daya felt them to be preliminary – was not very clear. Last year alone, he said reproachfully, half a dozen men from Kakrana had been picked up by the police. Some were released after a few days, others spent months in custody. And that was only one link in a whole chain of calamities. As for the Maoists:

'They live in the jungle, come and go as they please. They haven't asked for more than food and that was a long time ago. The police, on the other hand, accuse us of sheltering them, and that is wrong.'

'Well, I believe that if the Maoists were to ask for something, you'd have to give it to them – after all, they have guns too. But that is a different thing, a wider question. Let's return to the encounter...' Daya felt tired; he wanted to get to the point quickly.

There was silence.

'Did anybody see the police that day?' he asked conversationally.

'I did,' someone said from a corner. It was a young man with a sharp, mobile face and a wispy moustache; he wore a cloth knotted around his head in lieu of a turban.

'What did you see?'

'I ran into them while going to cut wood. They stopped me...'

'How many policemen?'

'About fifteen.'

'Did you notice the prisoners?'

'Yes, they had their hands bound.'

'What happened after that?'

'I showed them the way...they seemed on edge, nervous. Afterwards they told me to go back home. I didn't want to return to the ridge – some of them were waiting there – so I went by another path. On the way I heard gunfire.'

'What did you do after that?'

'I went home double-quick,' the man said, but the way he spoke betrayed a hint of constraint.

Daya remained silent. The man looked at the ground (he had spoken without getting up). A few words – sentences – in their own language were exchanged; they sounded like the light-toned chirping of birds. The young man raised his head.

'There's a place from where you can look down,' he said nervously. 'They were standing there with the bodies lying on the ground...'

'Thank you,' Daya said sincerely. 'Did any of you know Stephen Murmu?'

'I did,' the middle-aged peasant said without

hesitation. 'He came here: we met in the headman's house. He stayed the night and in the morning he went away.'

'Did you know that he'd been arrested?'

'No.'

Daya turned to the young man.

'Have you told your story to anyone?' he asked.

'No,' the man said uneasily. 'For a long time I kept what I'd seen to myself, my wife was the only one who knew. Some time ago we went to Murmu's widow and she…' He broke off.

The middle-aged peasant took up his sentence. 'She told us that you'd protect him – us.'

'I'll do my best,' Daya said quietly. 'The station officer has already been arrested. If you're willing to depose – sign a statement, that is – I'll undertake to keep it confidential for as long as possible. Think it over, there's no hurry.'

The peasant looked doubtful.

~

When Daya returned from Kakrana, the sergeant and Surab M'ta had also been placed under arrest. They were lodged in the guardhouse along with the station officer. Venkat sat placidly on a chair outside, smoking. The constables on duty watched him nervously from the corner of their eyes.

Daya spent the rest of the day questioning the sergeant and M'ta. The former, sweating blood, remained mute, but M'ta cracked in the end. However, he refused to sign a formal statement. Daya invited the station officer to reconsider his position in the light of M'ta's admission, but he answered glumly that he preferred to wait, adding that if *they* thought they could hang him out to dry, *they* were much mistaken.

It was after midnight when Daya went to bed. He was woken early in the morning by a telephone call from the director, apoplectic at a newspaper report he had just finished perusing. It summarized the progress of Daya's investigation, from the sensational confession of one of the policemen involved to the station officer's arrest, alluding to a chain of corruption that was rumoured to reach the very top of government.

A pretty kettle of fish, snarled the director. Did Daya have any idea of the damage this could cause?

Daya might have pointed to the blow-by-blow accounts that his colleagues were accustomed to giving *their* favoured journalists. Instead he apologized for his carelessness, stressing that his inquiries had reached a critical stage – the publicity might even do some good. The director retorted that publicity was precisely what he objected to, especially when the facts themselves were cloudy. Daya replied that he hoped to attain the requisite clarity shortly.

'Very well,' said the director. 'I'm prepared to back you – even at the cost of incurring some hostility. But from now on, I want no leaks and no flights of fancy. Get me hard evidence.'

Meanwhile, journalists and TV crews were descending upon the capital.

~

'The shit has hit the fan…I could say *I told you so*, but don't worry, I won't…no, I'm not blaming you: the essential thing is to keep a cool head… Is he likely to talk?'

'Never. He's as tough as they come.'

'That sounds like what you said about the southerner, that he wouldn't get anywhere and look where we are now…'

'You know yourself how far back we go – I've known the man for years.'

'Right now I'm guessing that he'll be worried about one thing and one thing only and that's how to save his own skin… Have you spoken to him?'

'Not after his arrest, no, but I'm working on it.'

'If the southerner could get that constable to confess, he could conceivably put enough pressure on your friend to make him talk. In that case I don't need to tell you what the consequences could be – for all of us.'

'What should we do?'

'Find some way of reaching him. Tell him it'll

take time – right now it's vital to let things quieten down. He'll be uncomfortable for a while, but in the end we'll get him out: the best lawyers, bail as soon as possible…provided, always provided he keeps his mouth shut.'

'All right.'

'What we need is time: let the damned southerner go first. We're working on it.'

'I understand.'

'Now for something strictly between ourselves. If the worst comes to the worst, remember the Telgi affair? Given a bit of time anything could happen: papers can vanish into thin air, a suspect fall ill, even die…do you understand what I mean?'

'I think so.'

'Good. We need cool heads – and strong stomachs. Remember that…'

~

'What do you think of the Kakrana affair?'

'A nine days wonder.'

'I agree. But I was referring to the investigation.'

'Well, the agency appears to be doing its job. Naturally I don't go into details...'

'It's precisely the details that worry me...no, let me finish. Have you considered the damage to the party? Not to mention other considerations...'

'Well?'

'Let me begin by saying that I don't question the officer's findings, not at all. The encounter may be false and it's quite possible he has proof of it. In that case, let the law take its course. Of course, in saying that, I'm discounting the other side of the question. I refer to our cumbersome legal procedures, their inadequacy when confronted with terrorist crimes. After all, no one disputes that the dead men were Maoists. To put Maoism down, strong measures are required... But, as I was saying, let's leave all that aside and go strictly by the book. What worries me – and should worry you too – is the conspiracy this officer, a southerner to boot, seems intent upon inventing, a conspiracy as chimerical as it is damaging. I don't mean the spectacle of a colleague arraigned by innuendo, without a shred of evidence, purely on the basis of hearsay. No, the damage is more serious in that it might affect the outcome of the next elections...'

'By antagonizing Reddy, you mean? I can't say I share your estimate of his importance. We're getting a bad press on corruption – that, if anything, could swing the election. Besides I don't know that Reddy has anything to complain of – no charges have been laid against him.'

'Aren't you being a bit disingenuous? What do you call this article about his proximity to certain interests suspected to be involved in the encounter, how and why God only knows?'

'That has nothing to do with the investigation. As long as Reddy hasn't been indiscreet, he's got nothing to worry about.'

'Except that this southerner is intent upon creating a full-blown scandal. He has the zeal of a rabid dog. To me he seems the kind of man who tries to prove his own rectitude by arraigning everyone else...a born troublemaker, in short. It amazes me that he was sent down there in the first place.'

'The agency assures me that he's being circumspect.'

'Would you call his actions circumspect? The man seems determined to chase every hare, however illusory. Let us say that Reddy is friendly with certain businessmen who've contributed generously to the party. Let us say that a company promoted by them wins a contract in fair competition. Can you imagine how that might be interpreted?'

'I see.'

'You know I have a certain regard for Reddy personally. Politically I believe that he is useful to us, especially at this juncture. Do try to restrain this officer's wilder fantasies. It would be even better to replace him since his investigation, for all practical purposes, has ended…'

~

It was a balmy morning. The hum of the city, filtered through the leafy precincts of the garden, amplified Daya's nagging, burning tiredness – the result of too many cigarettes, too little sleep. He had hurried to the capital, determined to strike while the iron was hot. Forewarned by instinct and experience, he could sense shadows gathering around the investigation.

Patnaik appeared in the doorway. Daya waved him into a chair.

'I believe that you can help us with our inquiry,' he began formally.

Patnaik crossed his legs and sat up straighter. His clothes were well cut and expensive. The smell of his aftershave was already arousing contradictory feelings in Venkat – a sense of respect mingled with rancour.

'I don't see how,' Patnaik said, in a voice from which he strove to expunge all traces of unease. Unsuccessfully. The deputy looked up, alert.

'I'll explain. As you know, we're investigating an incident in Kakrana in which two prisoners, supposedly Maoists, were killed while trying to escape. We were asked to verify the claim. During our investigation, we uncovered evidence showing that the men were in fact killed in cold blood… All very unfortunate, as I'm sure you'll agree.'

'It's unfortunate if true… The police are sometimes driven to excess by zeal.'

'You mean that they are sometimes driven to murder by zeal. The evidence was so strong that we arrested the officer responsible. As for zeal, it can be directed to things other than the performance of one's duties.'

'I don't understand.'

'You will in a minute. Now, why were these men killed? An obvious question, don't you think? The obvious answer is – because they were Maoists. Misplaced zeal, in short. However, one of them was a lawyer who happened to be involved in a peaceful campaign against mining. But mining, as you know, is a profitable business, especially when claims for damage can be evaded. I'm sure you're aware of the details.'

'I don't recollect offhand–'

'I can refresh your memory,' Daya reassured him. He handed Patnaik a piece of paper. 'This is the name of the station officer of Sirkhedi. Have you ever spoken to him?'

He's talked, thought Patnaik, and an icy shudder ran down his spine. He had been on tenterhooks ever since receiving Daya's summons, an anxiety only partially assuaged by the news, late at night, that the station officer had remained mute. He collected himself with an effort.

'I'm afraid I don't remember. One meets so many people.'

'I understand,' Daya said sympathetically. 'In the course of one's work…'

'That's so,' confirmed Patnaik, suspecting a trap.

'Still. Are you sure you haven't seen him recently?'

'No. And now that I come to think of it, I don't believe that I've met him at all.'

'That's curious,' Daya said. 'Very curious. For if you don't know him, why were you talking to him on the phone on these dates?'

Patnaik picked the paper up and pretended to study it. Daya was watching him – to Patnaik, his gaze seemed to express boundless derision and contempt.

'I remember now,' he said, and his voice unconsciously acquired a supplicating tinge. 'He did call up – it was about a transfer for someone, a relative or a friend. You know how it is…people ring up in support of petitions, requests.'

'Which you aim to satisfy, no doubt… This request – was it made by someone in your department?'

'I can't remember.'

'Can you remember the name at least?'

'I'm afraid not – I'm a busy man with many responsibilities…'

'So I gather,' said Daya, and there was a mocking edge to his voice. 'You'll notice that some of the calls are quite long. What did you talk about apart from this…request?'

'I don't remember. Mutual acquaintances perhaps…'

'So you had mutual acquaintances.'

Patnaik was floundering. Daya paused to give his discomfiture room to grow before returning to the attack.

'There's something else about these calls that strikes me as interesting...you see, we know exactly how many times he phoned you, along with the dates and the length of each call. Three of them were made on the very day I interrogated him. Not only that, they were placed in the interval between my interrogation and his arrest. A very odd coincidence, don't you think?'

Patnaik licked his lips. 'I don't know why he called me when he did,' he said haltingly. 'What we spoke about, I've already told you...'

'Curious, isn't it? That a man with so much on his mind – an accusation of murder, the threat of imminent arrest – should choose that precise moment to endorse a request for a transfer. As odd as something else we turned up. We took the precaution of vetting all the members of your household, servants included. In that way we learned that your driver has two telephone numbers registered in his name. When we asked him – confidentially, of course – he confessed that you had appropriated one of them for your own use…that you'd asked him to apply for it, in fact. Naturally, I looked up the call records. I assume I don't need to tell you what I found out…the number was used to ring the station officer up – don't worry, we're investigating the other calls you made from it as well. Not once or twice, but a great many times. One of the calls was made the day before he took the prisoners to Kakrana. Quite an exchange of courtesies, eh? You were careful, but not careful enough. You used a clandestine number to talk to him, but he called you up on your official number as well.'

'There's no law against keeping two numbers…'

'No,' Daya agreed. 'It's the calls made from them that I'm interested in.'

Patnaik's bearing had gone huddled and slack.

'All right,' he said. 'I know the station officer, I admit it. I wanted to keep it dark for professional reasons. I did talk to him, but it was only about some land I wanted to buy in Sirkhedi…I swear it.'

'Ah, your investments…I was about to come to that. The list is already quite extensive, wouldn't you say?'

'What's that?' Patnaik asked dully as yet another piece of paper was placed before him.

'A list of your assets. This is just what we've managed to uncover so far, no doubt there's more. It adds up to an impressive pile: two apartments and a plot of land here in the capital; a house and an empty lot in your home town. Farmland – quite a lot of it – bought at different times. You've been a bureaucrat all your life: how does one amass that kind of fortune?'

'I made some lucky investments…'

'Miraculous, I'd say. And we haven't even come to the most interesting item: five thousand shares in a mining company, bought in your wife's name. The same company that has been awarded a lucrative lease on the plateau. A small investment, less than two per cent of its paid-up capital, but with the potential of making you a millionaire several times over…it also makes you an accessory to murder.'

'What do you mean?'

'The calls you exchanged with the station officer prove that you planned the encounter in cahoots with him. We'll get his confession soon – he's already made it clear that he doesn't plan to go quietly into the good night. But you know that already…'

At his feet, Patnaik could see a black pit yawning. 'What do you want?' he asked dully, and even before finishing the question he knew what the answer would be. But a terror greater than that of the pit kept him from confessing. Daya had some inkling of it, but no way of guessing its strength.

'I want the names of the men who ordered Ghandy and Murmu killed,' he said. 'I'm quite prepared to believe that you were only a messenger. But I need names, circumstantial details. You know as well as I do that they'll gladly hang you out to dry…if, on the other hand, you've nothing to say, you can face the music alone. It makes no difference to me.'

'There's no one,' said Patnaik, sweating.

Now is the time to turn the screw, thought Daya. A few days in prison will knock the stuffing out of him. All his life, he's believed himself invulnerable. Reduced to the condition of a vagrant, a common convict, someone to whom anything at all might happen, he'll break… But I don't have a warrant, and even if I did, he'd obtain quite as much reassurance in prison as in his own house. No, I'll have to let him go.

'All right,' he said aloud. 'In that case, I'm going to hold you in custody for further questioning.'

It was eleven in the morning.

~

'Patnaik has squealed.'

The station officer looked up dully. 'What?' he said.

'You heard me…your friend has talked. I can see it doesn't surprise you. How did we get him? In the simplest way possible – all those phone calls were incautious to say the least. When I pointed that out to Patnaik, he agreed. Don't blame him; he hasn't your experience in bumping people off. Which means he'll get a lighter sentence. Unless you can show that you acted under orders. I'm not asking for documents, that would be expecting too much. Your word will do… The other thing about Patnaik is that he has so much more to lose. "Assets disproportionate to known sources of income" is the technical term – wildly disproportionate in his case. And yours. Here, take a look.'

The station officer looked at the paper.

'This guarantees you'll lose your job. So will Patnaik, but his fall is more damaging. You see, he thinks of himself as being not just respectable but respected, with lots of connections and important friends. Who'll drop him faster than you can blink an eye. No cushy deputations, no foreign trips, no directorships and junkets…it hit him hard, as you can imagine. So he confessed. Only he says it was your idea, that he tried to talk you out of it, suggest something less…drastic. But you wouldn't listen.'

'You're lying.'

'How do you think I dug this up? And knowing Patnaik, what on earth makes you think he wouldn't talk? He sang like a bird – he even told me about B.S.K. Do you know him? Of course you do. A businessman with a finger in every pie, even mining. But that's neither here nor there. The point is, what are you going to do now?'

The station officer was thinking rapidly. As the emotions flitted across his unguarded face, Daya had no difficulty interpreting them: alarm and rage, followed by resignation. Oddly enough, the station officer harboured no doubts that Patnaik had actually confessed – Daya had taken care to have him brought to the office the previous evening to answer a few meaningless questions and obtain a good view of the supposed prisoner.

The news of Patnaik's arrest left the station officer thoughtful and shaken. After a night passed in panic-stricken conjectures, he was ready to believe anything. The initials tossed out casually, like a scrap of meat, were the clinching straw. There was no way the southerner could know about B.S.K. unless Patnaik had talked (here the station officer underestimated Daya's resourcefulness). At that instant he would have been prepared to believe that his own mother had testified against him.

'All right,' he said, so huskily that Daya had to strain to hear. 'All right,' he repeated, louder this time. 'If that bastard, that son of a bitch, hasn't had the good manners to remain silent, I'll tell you the truth. I killed those men, at least I arranged for them to be killed, but that was because Patnaik asked me. I know him, we go back a long way: he's done me favours and I've repaid them. If he thinks that he can fix me and get away with it, I'll repay that too...Murmu was making a nuisance of himself, had been for a long time. Patnaik was worried. So I had the idea of putting Murmu away for a while, to cool him down – purely as a favour to Patnaik. He jumped at it – said he'd make it worth my while. So I arrested Murmu and worked him over. Soon after that, Shanker was arrested. One day, I get a call from Patnaik suggesting I have them put away permanently – he says he's counting on me. The next day I get another call – I'm not going to tell you his name, he hasn't sold me down the river – saying that the only good Maoist is a dead Maoist... And that's how they repay me – by leaving me to carry the can!'

'Who are Patnaik's friends?'

'I don't know...ask him. As far as I'm concerned, Patnaik told me what to do and I did it.'

Daya leaned back in his chair. His deputy shuffled the papers on which he had been writing and placed them before the station officer. He hesitated, seized a pen, and signed quickly and nervously.

~

Daya called the director to acquaint him with the station officer's confession. He listened silently and authorized a warrant for Patnaik's arrest (who was at home in his own bed, tossing in disjointed sleep, troubled by bad dreams). Things were about to get much worse, as he would discover when a policeman arrived with a warrant for his arrest at the crack of dawn. He was taken to Daya's temporary office pale and trembling. Before Daya could begin questioning him, he collapsed into a chair, clutching his chest and complaining of a heart condition. The inspector would have pressed on regardless if a lawyer hadn't arrived in the nick of time. In the end Patnaik was ferried to hospital, saving him from the ordeal of an immediate interrogation to which his nerves were clearly unequal.

Daya left Venkat in the hospital with instructions to allow no one access to the prisoner except the doctor on duty. A specialist was summoned: he spoke sombrely of the patient's medical history and recommended complete rest. How many calls had it taken, Daya wondered grimly, to persuade him? Just one, probably. Daya was certain that

Patnaik was perfectly healthy, if scared out of his wits. Fuming, he returned to his office where he found Kemat waiting for him. It was a welcome distraction.

Kemat had just returned from a students' demonstration which had been broken up by the police. They spoke of the Maoists, of Kemat's cousin who had joined them and whom he had not met for years. After a while Daya felt like a drink. Kemat offered to get rice beer from a nearby shebeen.

'I'll come with you,' said Daya. 'Can we drink there?'

Kemat assured him that the place was perfectly clean.

'It doesn't matter,' said Daya indifferently. 'Let's go.'

They walked through tree-shaded avenues to a shabby neighbourhood that petered out into wasteland, with scattered hovels and tiny patches of cultivation. Dirt paths snaked through this urban wilderness, a seam in the patchwork of slums pushing into the countryside. Here the city seemed to waver and vanish but it was only an illusion. Scraps of plastic and cloth, empty bottles and disintegrating chappals littered the ground, from which rose the faint whiff of excrement.

Kemat halted at a hut near a spreading acacia tree: it was set in a courtyard of beaten earth plastered with cow dung. A light bulb with its draggle of wire hung from a pole stuck into the ground. 'This is it,' said Kemat and disappeared into the doorway. He emerged holding two bottles. They drank, sitting on plastic chairs. The netted foliage of the thorn tree was picked out in bronze where the light fell upon it. Then they walked back to the road where Daya hailed a rickshaw. Back in his room, he lay down and collapsed into a dreamless sleep.

~

'It looks bad.'

'What d'you mean, bad? It's disastrous.'

'All right...it looks disastrous.'

'This is no time for joking...I spoke to Patnaik. Fortunately he had the sense to fall ill, otherwise there's no knowing what might have happened...'

'Doesn't Patnaik realize they can't do anything to him? He's better protected than I am!'

'He's soft, his nerves are weak.'

'We've had bad luck all the way down the line. One forgets how dangerous an honest cop can be...'

'But what about Patnaik? How can we get him off now that the idiot – yes, you're right, an idiot – has confessed? *And what if we can't?*'

'There are no two ways about it – either we protect Patnaik or take drastic measures. Oddly enough, that's exactly what I told him when we were discussing his downy friend's predicament. However, let us exhaust the other possibilities first.'

'What do you mean?'

'Firstly, we mustn't let the southerner dig any further; secondly, we must discredit the evidence he's obtained already. The crux, as I understand it, is the evidence against the station officer. What an idiot to leave so many loose ends lying about! And to confess out of spite, pure and simple spite. And Patnaik claimed that he was as tough as they come... But the situation hasn't changed: if we can prove his innocence, it doesn't matter how many times he spoke to Patnaik – they could have been talking about whores, property deals or the man in the moon for all anyone cares...'

'But what about his confession? And Khartiya's confession?'

'I was coming to that. Since when did confessions become sacraments? People make them all the time, only to take them back – the honest and dishonest both. The only reason it can't be done in this case is that Khartiya is dead. But the station officer – that son of a bitch – is alive, very much so, and he'll take his confession back if it's the last thing he does. Anyway, time enough to make him tell his beads once we've wriggled out of this hole... The solution is simple:

we'll have to disprove Khartiya's confession.'

'How? The man is dead.'

'There's more than one way of skinning a cat. Let us suppose he made it to settle a score, or, better still, because he was unbalanced mentally, subject to some kind of mania… What would it be worth then? Nothing, precisely nothing.'

'But how do we prove that?'

'Find a doctor – a local man, well respected, someone whose word no one will dream of doubting. Get him to say that Khartiya came to him – or was brought to him. That he diagnosed him as suffering from delusions, persecution mania. That's why Khartiya was sent on leave – unfortunately he killed himself before his treatment could begin…'

'It's an idea.'

'Get him to forge case papers. Rig some evidence to corroborate the story – put pressure on Khartiya's colleagues, his family…it's a matter of the right inducement, a few threats. Once his sanity is called into question it's an easy matter to cast doubt upon his confession. At the very least, it will muddy the waters; enough, anyway, to get the station officer off. As for *his* confession, he can say that he was tortured – physically, psychologically, it doesn't matter. Corrupt maybe, but blameless of murder…'

'And would a judge believe that?'

'That's a lawyer's business. In any case, it gives us a fighting chance. Especially if we can get the southerner removed. That opens the door to an arrangement with his successor – they aren't all like that in the agency, you know. On the contrary.'

'You think on your feet.'

'And why? Because I know something your tender years have yet to learn: in this country there's almost nothing you can't get away with *if you keep your nerve*. Remember that. Here, everyone is looking to buy or sell something – information, influence, jobs, contracts, daughters. Only the stupid and foolhardy get caught. Intelligence, on the other hand, involves knowing when to draw your head in and when to attack…

You've seen flocks of sheep driven south in winter, haven't you? Of course you have – they hold up the traffic and no one, as usual, gives a damn. A single herdsman drives a mob of hundreds. It's reflex that keeps them together – breaking away would be against the natural order of things. Well, we're the herdsmen, you and I – it's just a matter of skill...'

~

'Now that everything else has been sorted out, let us talk about the Kakrana case.'

'What about it?'

'There was a rumpus in parliament today – the usual stuff, the opposition accusing us of shielding the corrupt... I find it ironic, considering that the investigation is proceeding vigorously, far too vigorously in my opinion. As far as I can make out, there's no evidence linking Reddy to the case in any way.'

'Reddy isn't being investigated; nor is there

anything to warrant such an investigation as far as I know...'

'What about the summons to his son?'

'I didn't know that.'

'You didn't? I'm relieved to hear that, my dear fellow. I thought you were going out on a limb over this one. Unfortunately, the press is having a field day. I agree that it's good for our image to be seen cracking down on corruption, but things can very easily get out of hand... In that case everybody risks being tarred with the same brush – Reddy, me, you...'

'I don't think things have gone as far as that.'

'The inquiry is taking in a lot of things along the way, isn't it? Too many if you ask me. Take the notion that Patnaik is involved – it strains one's credulity, at least it strains mine. He may have accepted money, but how many of us haven't succumbed to temptation at one time or another? It's human nature... Besides, what's the harm in smoothing a transaction that would have occurred in any case? But these are hypothetical matters – from accusing a man of corruption to accusing him of murder is a large leap. And what does this southerner do? Why, he begins raking over Patnaik's friends and associates, making an inventory of his phone calls. Good heavens, a man in that position is bound to be in touch with any number of people in business, politics, government. Supposing I call him up to ask about an official decision, quite informally, mind you, or to sound him about some aspect of policy…does that mean I'm complicit in his supposed crimes?'

'I'm told that there is substantial evidence against Patnaik. The station officer's confession, for one thing…'

'That confession… It strikes me, my dear fellow, that confessions have to be upheld in court. Badger a man long enough and he'll confess to anything you want. Maybe the station officer doesn't like the cut of Patnaik's jib. Do you really think that Patnaik, or anyone else in his position, would get his hands dirty in that way? The risk, the risk! As for the other thing, let he who is without sin cast the first stone. If you really start going after the corrupt, how many of our own people would be left in government? Even an honest man must wink at a certain amount of dishonesty. It's the system, human nature, in short… In any case, let Patnaik explain where he got his money from. But from that to murder is a leap in the dark if you ask me. And one fraught with unintended consequences.'

'What do you mean?'

'Political consequences, administrative ones. When the Maoists attack the police we're criticized for not doing enough to support our men in uniform. When the police adopt tough measures, we're criticized for letting them take the law into their own hands. It's demoralizing all around…'

'I see.'

'The situation is causing concern in the highest quarters: there's a feeling that things are getting out of hand. Naturally, no one would dream of encroaching upon your jurisdiction…'

'What would you suggest?'

'An end to the uncertainty. Let the agency present its evidence. Procrastination may be a virtue sometimes, but not when the sword is hanging over our own heads. Even if we admit that the inquiry might be useful in keeping Reddy in line until the elections, there's the media to consider. Industry already sees it as a witch-hunt – you should read some of the letters I've been getting. It's time to put a lid on things.'

~

An innocuous spring day. Daya looked out of the window, feeling bored and tense; he had been waiting in the antechamber for half an hour. When he was finally waved in, the first thing he saw was the back of the minister's head. The chair turned and an affable countenance with stony eyelids emerged from its depths.

'Sit down,' Reddy said.

Daya sat down – as though at a game he didn't much care for but was determined not to lose all the same. The minister came to the point at once.

'I asked to meet you in connection with the Kakrana case.'

'So I gathered.'

'About your summons to my son… On what basis are you accusing him?'

'We haven't accused him of anything. I'm just looking for answers.'

'Answers to what? My son is a businessman.'

'It's his business dealings I'm interested in.'

'Be careful, Inspector – don't overreach yourself.'

'I assume your son has told you what I want to know. You could clear it up just as well as he.'

'Are you accusing me too?

'I wouldn't dream of it…I'm merely asking you for the answers your son refused to give.'

'Which are?'

'The reason why a company promoted by your family was granted a valuable mining concession recently. I assume you're aware of it.'

'Why don't you refresh my memory?'

'Gladly. I've written its name here on this piece of paper. Along with a chart showing its shareholders. Two charts actually. One with the names of the people who set it up – I presume you recognize them?'

'D'you think I'm in the habit of denying my friends? He's a friend of mine.'

'Exactly. The second chart shows some interesting changes. A large block of shares is transferred – through an offshore transaction – to a company owned by your son. This transfer occurs soon after the auction for certain mining rights is held, an auction in which the company wins a large and valuable lease.'

'What interests you about this transaction?'

'Many things…its timing, for one; the fact that you were in office when the company won the bid; the fact that Patnaik also holds a stake in it. I asked your son about these…coincidences, but he could give me no satisfactory answer.'

'Perhaps because they're nothing but a figment of your imagination. My son is a businessman in touch with other businessmen: like them he looks for avenues of investment. It was a business opportunity, offered by a friend who could have gone elsewhere. A question of friendship, in short.'

'And Patnaik's stake – was that a question of friendship too?'

'You can ask him – you have him in custody. I understand perfectly well what you're trying to do – pull me down through my son… My political opponents would like nothing better. But the fact remains that he had nothing to do with the encounter and you won't be able to prove otherwise, however much you browbeat Patnaik.'

'The station officer's confession–'

'That confession… It strikes me, Inspector, that there are too many confessions floating about. How you extracted them remains an open question.'

'I'm gratified by your belief in my ability to browbeat a man accustomed to doing quite a bit of browbeating himself… However, let us put the encounter aside and concentrate on the company. Don't you think the timing of the transfer suggests a quid pro quo?'

'I think nothing of the kind.'

'Why go to such lengths to disguise your stake in that case?'

'Any accountant would tell you that – for tax purposes.'

'What else? However, given the position that you hold…'

'You're joking – the chief minister would dearly like to have me removed, as you doubtless know, better than anyone else. Let us be frank. You're an honest officer, I don't doubt that, but you're being used. Maybe you don't know that, but it's true. Contracts, bids are complicated things – I'm minister for home, my responsibilities are law and order. What do you expect me to say to my son – give up a profitable deal just because I'm in office? As for that encounter for which you're willing to destroy a man's career – do you know how many people are killed by the Maoists every year? What are the police supposed to do, applaud? D'you know what the plateau is like? Wretched, poverty-ridden, with hardly any roads, electricity, schools. A people backward and ignorant beyond belief. It's mines that'll bring prosperity there, but you'd prefer the police to run away and the mines not to open, eh?'

'What I'd prefer is neither here nor there. You may not think much of these coincidences, but as far as I'm concerned they're a criminal matter.'

Reddy recited a Sanskrit verse. 'Do you know what that means?' he asked. 'It's from the Gita, about the duties proper to one's station. A warrior's duty is not the same as a farmer's...don't concern yourself with my duties, Inspector.'

'All in all, I don't agree,' Daya said.

~

The next day's newspapers described how the honourable minister had asked to meet Inspector Dayanidhi of the agency in order to answer any questions that he might have. Reddy emphasized that he had taken this unorthodox step to dispel the unjustified rumours swirling around his son, who was entirely blameless – as any accountant would testify. He accused the agency of conducting a witch-hunt founded on tenuous indications and outrageous suspicions, of illegally widening the scope of its inquiry and sweeping all and sundry into its orbit. He hoped that those unjustly accused would soon be exonerated and that the climate of fear created by the agency would not affect investments in a region the government had taken such pains to open up. Meanwhile, he congratulated the police on their zeal in combating the scourge of Maoism.

Daya read the report gloomily. At the director's insistence he had filed a charge sheet, but his determination to push forward with his inquiries remained unabated.

But a few days later he was forced to put them aside in the face of evidence purporting to show that Khartiya had been mentally unbalanced at the time of making his deposition. According to an affidavit filed by the senior doctor in the government hospital in Badalpur, Khartiya had come to see him, accompanied by a friend, complaining of sleeplessness and strange hallucinations. After examining him, the doctor had diagnosed incipient schizophrenia. This diagnosis was communicated to the station officer and Khartiya granted leave with immediate effect.

In support of this contention were statements by Jairam Awasiya and Khartiya's father testifying to evident changes in the young man's behaviour for some time. Needless to say, the station officer had changed his tune and was warbling about his own suspicions. Ratified by the doctor's report, they had induced him to grant Khartiya leave on compassionate grounds. A medical certificate was not asked for in the hope that he would be cured quietly, without the stigma of mental illness appearing in his service record. The station officer explained that he had omitted to mention this earlier out of resentment at the inspector's bullying tactics – no, he preferred to let the truth emerge by itself.

Daya's first response was to summon Khartiya's father. Did he realize, he demanded harshly, what he was doing? Did he actually intend to shield those who had driven his son to suicide?

The old man remained mute.

'Well?'

He mumbled that they were poor, ignorant folk – was it their fault that Jagdish had killed himself?

'He should have thought of us. Anyhow, what's past is past – the dead are gone. It's better to think of the living instead.'

'What did they promise you?'

Silence. Daya felt like seizing the old man by the shoulders and shaking the answer out of him.

'Answer me,' he said quietly, and something in his tone made Khartiya's father quail.

'They promised to take his brother in his place.'

'On compassionate grounds... Wasn't Awasiya your son's friend?'

'Yes.'

'What did *he* get?'

The old man said nothing. Daya dismissed him.

After he had scurried out, Daya fell to musing blackly upon that lodestar of Indian life, the family. Of the crimes committed in its name, the dead sacrificed to it. Nothing can be done for them – 'better to think of the living instead'. Arguments born out of desperation, greed and twisted notions of honour.

His bitter reflections were interrupted by the arrival of Murmu's widow. She had dropped in to learn the progress of the case. She told him of the salutary effects of the station officer's arrest – the climate of fear and intimidation in Sirkhedi had lightened perceptibly. Daya kept his thoughts to himself.

'What will you do now?' he asked her.

She remained silent. Marry again, she might have said, had she known him better. And find out why we couldn't have children. Although that was lucky in the end.

Daya tried to explain that his inquiry had come

up against an unexpected obstruction. She showed no surprise.

'I'm doing my best,' Daya added hastily.

Bleakly, he wondered whether it would ever be enough. The testimony of one expert would be cancelled by the objections of another. A climate of fear would keep the honest from testifying. And without Khartiya's confession, what would happen to the edifice he had painstakingly built up?

'It doesn't look good,' he said unwillingly.

'It doesn't matter,' she said.

'Of course it does.'

'I only meant that things go wrong sometimes for no fault of our own. Although I'd be very sorry to see anyone from Kakrana get into trouble… after all, I persuaded them to come forward.'

'I was wondering about that – how did you manage it?'

'It wasn't too difficult…'

'As to that you can rest easy. I was keeping their testimony in reserve for the trial.'

'That's all right then.'

'What about your husband?' Daya asked her.

'There are some things that can't be helped,' she said.

Do you really think so, Daya wanted to ask. That the station officer and all his ilk are facts of nature, like drought or illness?

'Not that I like it,' she added, looking at him levelly.

'Where are you staying?' he asked.

'With a relative.'

'Can I walk you there?'

She glanced at him with surprise.

'All right.'

But he took her to the institute instead. There, in the garden, he told her the whole story from beginning to end.

'Stephen knew him,' she said when he had finished.

'Who?'

'Khartiya – some of the constables aren't too bad, you know. He came to our house a few times, he seemed a nice man.'

'I see,' Daya said, not knowing what else to say. After a pause, he added, 'I'm sorry, I've let you down…it was my job to find enough evidence to bring the guilty to trial. I owe you an apology.'

'You know, you're the first policeman I've met who's sorry for *not* doing his job… Well, you tried your best.'

'That doesn't matter,' Daya said bleakly.

They sat in silence. 'I should be going now,' she said after a while.

Supposing I put my arm around her, Daya thought, would she let me? She's vulnerable, lonely…what did she think of her husband? Did she love him? What kind of man does she like? But between them lay an abyss that could not be bridged – he had a horror of abusing his position. A young woman with small breasts and hips, thoughtful, accepting life's hardships (though not all of them, fortunately). She stirred.

'Do you have family?' she asked.

'A mother, a sister...'

'No wife?'

'And no children either.'

'Neither do I,' she said simply.

'Does it bother you – not having children?'

'It marks one out. Besides, there are other... difficulties. It's safer to have a home of one's own.'

'Your husband was a good man...I'm sorry.'

'Yes, well, life goes on.'

'Here, take this.' Daya gave her his card. 'If you get into trouble, any trouble at all – especially with the police – call me.'

'All right,' she said.

Perhaps there was more to be said, but he could not for the life of him think of it. Twilight was falling, thinning the garden out, absorbing it into shadow – a rose bush, a flowering magnolia, the gulmohar boxing the sky above their heads. The lines of darkness were drawing taut. A nightjar called anxiously, a sunbird skittered away and was sucked into the momentary hush. The sky had a faint sheen as though of pearl – bats flitted across its surface, shadows joining shadows.

'Let's go,' he said irresolutely.

~

A few days later Daya was assigned to another case – this gave him the dubious consolation of watching his defeat from a distance. It was not so much the personal element that rankled but the fact that justice had been within reach before vanishing (like a mirage) as the impunity of crimes reasserted itself. He submitted a meticulous report outlining the case he had built up, the whole chain of reasoning that ran from the station officer to Reddy, the evidence to be marshalled to disprove Khartiya's insanity, lines of inquiry that remained incomplete. He kept a copy with the vague idea of leaking it to the press if all else failed.

After which silence supervened. The investigation remained in abeyance; his report vanished into that odourless, invisible inferno of dust where bureaucratic truths are consigned. Patnaik and the station officer applied for bail.

Daya's new case in a southern city took up most of his time. He was in Hyderabad when a copy of the final charge sheet arrived – incoherent, studded with procedural errors, his refutation of Khartiya's insanity irretrievably mangled. The document was a virtual guarantee that the station officer would be exonerated. With bitter lucidity Daya foresaw the collapse of all his hopes.

He should have become accustomed to losing. Yet it disturbed him profoundly. Try as he might, Daya could not prevent himself from slipping into a slough of rage and dejection under the burden of an unjustified guilt. Which was partly why he decided to make a detour of 500 kilometres on his way back in order to visit Binda, who was said to live in a village 'like a hermit'. For many years now they had made plans to meet, plans that came to nothing – until now.

He found Binda and his wife living simply,

though not in the least like hermits. The villagers, confided Binda, regarded him as an eccentric who had wasted his education. No one read his books, which were disqualified from consideration because they made no money. If his wife hadn't helped some weavers set up a cooperative they would have been harassed in all kinds of petty ways. Binda ran an informal school for their children. Everyone wanted English lessons but he refused to give any.

Binda regarded his neighbours as dupes of a consumer culture in which their aspirations were embedded like flies in aspic. But he refused to romanticize traditional culture with its inequalities and cruelties either. The countryside was full of problems and they did what they could simply because they lived there and felt responsible. For what? Everything – poverty, droughts, the lack of toilets. They had settled here because they loved the landscape, said Sara, and look what they had been drawn into.

After dinner Daya told them about his case,

sitting on the steps of the house under the stars, luminous and tranquil, seething with demonic fire, an unimaginable energy. 'Poor man,' Sara said when he had finished, and he did not ask whom she meant, Stephen Murmu or Jagdish Khartiya.

'What will happen now?' asked Binda.

'Nothing...things go back to normal, or what passes for normal.'

'That doesn't sound hopeful. You know, I never understood why you became a policeman.'

'Because a lawyer's job seemed too boring.'

'I read an article by a policeman recently,' Binda went on, ignoring the interruption. 'On the lines of: Don't the police have rights too? ... "Look at me, I'm a pleb," he says. "All my life I've been discriminated against." An irony considering the variety of oppressors our society throws up...'

'So?' asked Daya.

'Here's a man who advocates murder and torture as legitimate methods of defending the state, and yet he insists on calling it democratic.'

'Perhaps that's why I became a policeman.'

'Well, throw it up. Buy some land here – we'll help you. Read, grow things, write an exposé...'

'Tend my garden like Candide, you mean?'

'Perhaps. I've a feeling that we're headed for a crash. I don't mean the human race in general, though that's probably true as well, but–'

'Why do you think we can escape?' Sara objected.

'We can't. And why should we try? We're all involved, all implicated. But when the crash comes, it might be useful to remain close to the ground.'

'No,' Daya said. 'Not yet anyway. But isn't it incredible what happens, what keeps on happening?'

'Incredible?' Binda said judiciously. 'Perhaps not.'

'Well, if you adopt the viewpoint of the cosmos or the whole sweep of human history there's nothing to be said. Still, there are degrees of imperfection – why palliate the worst because the best is unattainable? In the end, we're saddled with the burden of what's here and now.'

'Or its possibilities.'

'Let us say both.'

Sara told him the story of a woman from their village who'd been diagnosed with heart trouble. She was sent to a public hospital in the city, where they told her that an operation would have to be performed. She waited for a month. After the operation, she had to sleep on a mattress in the corridor because all the beds were full. But the dispensary was empty and none of the nurses – women like herself – would consent to touch her until they were given a gratuity.

'There's nothing surprising in that,' Binda said.

'That's just the trouble,' Daya said sombrely.

He woke early the next morning and went for a walk. A touch of cold lingered in the air. Behind a bank of trees the sky's forge was brightening from orange to gold. He walked for a long time, trying to cast off the burden of his case with its unredressed balance of injustice and pain. He was feeling less dejected after last night's conversation, a bit calmer, though still febrile.

Returning, he paused to watch a bird that fluttered at the edge of his vision in a field planted with corn. Trees with pale yellowish trunks grew in one corner. It was there that he spotted the flycatcher, a delicate blotch of aquamarine. As he watched, it darted like an arrow to the green cornfield and came to rest upon a tree. Then it rose again, as though flung into the air, and returned in a swift dipping arc to the yellow grove – where it hovered momentarily, a whirr of blue, before vanishing from sight.

Afterword

I owe a debt to certain cherished writers – Stendhal, Tolstoy, George Eliot, Patrick White, Leonardo Sciascia. Occasionally I've made it explicit by paraphrasing a line or echoing a phrase read elsewhere.

A word about the dialogue. Some readers may object that my characters sound too British (or American) to be entirely convincing. In which case, they're invited to regard the book as being, partly at least, translated from an Indian language – any Indian language – as a way of getting around the difficulty. This useful pretence will allow them to imagine some people in it as speaking (and thinking) in English, while others talk to each other in a language that has been translated colloquially in the interests of naturalism.

I've aimed at realism in terms of texture, but mixed with the surreal, or fantastic. Amongst the surreal elements are Daya *and* the agency for which he works. Someone like him would be impossible to find in the ranks of the police in any country, not just India. I've put him down as an exemplar of the conscientious functionary, whose numbers anywhere are nowhere near enough.

The setting has deliberately been left unlocalized, imaginary – it could be any state or region in India at any time during the past fifteen or twenty years. And not just India either – the book can (I hope) be read as a fable about power and corruption, and the complicity that shapes their perverse labyrinths, anywhere. Needless to say, no one in it bears any resemblance to anybody real, living or dead (although it is almost impossible for invention to outdo reality). The same applies to its central event, the encounter. Although similar events keep occurring. Unfortunately.

Shashank Kela

Acknowledgements

I owe a debt of gratitude to Pankaj Mishra for support and encouragement; to Peter Straus for keeping faith; R. Sivapriya and Indra Das for their tact and forbearance (and for shepherding the book so capably to press); friends in India and elsewhere, who shall remain unnamed; family – and, above all, to Karuna, Mahil and Lyra.

A Note on the Author

Shashank Kela worked in a rural trade union of adivasi peasants for some years after graduating from university. Since 2010 he has written on history, politics, current affairs, ecology, and train travel (amongst other things). *The Other Man* is his first novel.

AN EXTENSIVE LIBRARY

Fresh new original Juggernaut books from the likes of Sunny Leone, Twinkle Khanna, Rujuta Diwekar, William Dalrymple, Pankaj Mishra, Arundhati Roy and lots more. Plus, books from partner publishers and all the free classics you want.

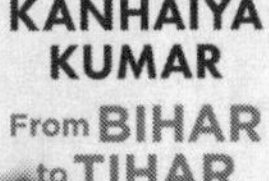

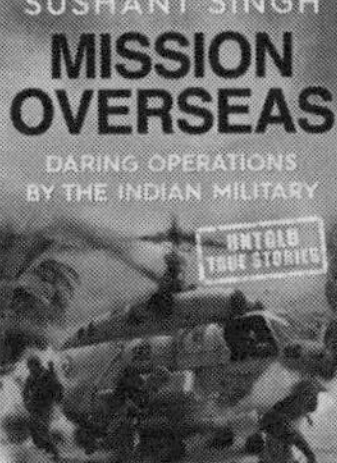

www.juggernaut.in

DON'T JUST READ; INTERACT

We're changing the reading experience from passive to active.

Ask authors questions

Get all your answers from the horse's mouth. Juggernaut authors actually reply to every question they can.

Rate and review

Let everyone know of your favourite reads or critique the finer points of a book – you will be heard in a community of like-minded readers.

Gift books to friends

For a book-lover, there's no nicer gift than a book personally picked. You can even do it anonymously if you like.

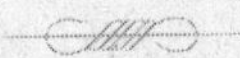

Enjoy new book formats

Discover serials released in parts over time, picture books including comics, and story-bundles at discounted rates.

www.juggernaut.in

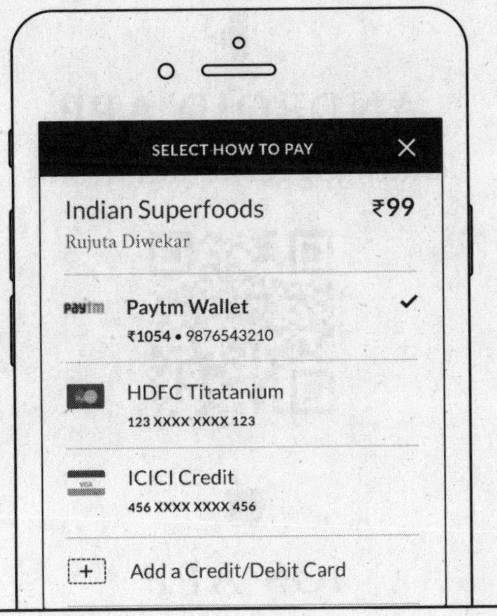

Paytm Wallet, Cards & Apple Payments

On Android, just add a Paytm Wallet once and buy any book with one tap. On iOS, pay with one tap with your iTunes-linked debit/credit card.

Click the QR Code with a QR scanner app or type the link into the Internet browser on your phone to download the app.

ANDROID APP

bit.ly/juggernautandroid

iOS APP

bit.ly/juggernautios